Louisa May Alcott (18? Pennsylvania, and grew Massachusetts. She received father, Bronson Alcott, a renowned educator and writer, as well as from Ralph Waldo Emerson and Henry David Thoreau, who were family friends. In 1868 she became editor of the children's magazine *Merry's Museum* and published the first volume of *Little Women*, a novel about four young sisters growing up in a small New England town during the Civil War. *Little Women* was one of the first American novels to become a classic in children's literature. It remains one of the best-loved books for girls.

"Recently I revisited *Little Women*, a book I'd read perhaps three dozen times in childhood. Reading again from a perspective of adulthood, I saw the profound influence this book has had on my morals, my values, my longing, and my dreams. When I stood at Louisa May Alcott's grave in Concord, Massachusetts, several months ago, I thanked her again for shaping my thoughts and thus shaping my life."—Karen Wojahn, as quoted in *Creative Writing: For People Who Can't Not Write* by Kathryn Lindskoog.

LITTLE WOMEN

Book One
Four Funny Sisters

Louisa May Alcott

Edited and abridged
by Kathryn Lindskoog

Illustrated by Barbara Chitouras

MULTNOMAH

Portland, Oregon 97266

Edited by Rodney L. Morris
Illustrations by Barbara Chitouras
Cover design by Durand Demlow

LITTLE WOMEN, BOOK ONE
This abridged edition
© 1991 by Kathryn Lindskoog
Published by Multnomah Press
10209 SE Division Street
Portland, Oregon 97266

Multnomah Press is a ministry of Multnomah School of the Bible,
8435 NE Glisan Street, Portland, Oregon 97220.

Printed in the United States of America.

Library of Congress Cataloging-in-Publication Data
Lindskoog, Kathryn Ann.
  Little women / Louisa May Alcott : edited and abridged by Kathryn Lindskoog
    p.   cm.
  Contents: Bk. 1. Four funny sisters – Bk. 2. The sisters grow up.
  Summary: An abridged retelling of the classic novel, chronicling the joys and sorrows of the four March sisters as they grow into young ladies in nineteenth-century New England.
  ISBN 0-88070-437-3(V.1) 0-88070-463-2(V.2)
  [1. Family life–Fiction. 2. Sisters–Fiction. 3. New England–Fiction.] I. Alcott, Louisa May, 1832-1888. Little women. II. Title.
PZ7.L147Li 1991   91-2739
[Fic]–dc20   CIP
                                                                      AC
            91 92 93 94 95 96 97 98 - 10 9 8 7 6 5 4 3 2 1

CONTENTS

1
PLAYING PILGRIMS

"CHRISTMAS WON'T BE CHRISTMAS without any presents," grumbled Jo, lying on the rug.

"It's so dreadful to be poor!" sighed Meg, looking down at her old dress.

"I don't think it's fair for some girls to have plenty of pretty things, and other girls nothing at all," added little Amy, with an injured sniff.

"We've got Father and Mother and each other," said Beth contentedly from her corner.

The four young faces in the firelight brightened at Beth's cheerful words, but darkened again as Jo said sadly, "We haven't got Father, and shall not have him for a long time." She didn't say "perhaps never," but each silently added it, thinking of Father far away, where the fighting was.

Nobody spoke for a minute, then Meg said, "You know the reason Mother proposed not having any presents this Christmas was because it is going to be a hard winter for everyone. She thinks we ought not spend money for pleasure when our men are suffering in the army. We can't do much, but we can make our little sacrifices gladly. But I am afraid I don't." And she shook her head, as she thought regretfully of all the pretty things she wanted.

"But I don't think the little we could spend would do any good. We've each got a dollar, and the army wouldn't be much helped by our giving that. I agree not to expect anything from Mother or you, but I do want to buy a new book for myself. I've wanted it *so* long," said Jo, who was a bookworm.

"I planned to spend mine on new music," said Beth, with a little sigh, which no one heard.

"I shall get a nice box of Faber's drawing pencils. I really need them," said Amy decidedly.

"Mother didn't say anything about our money, and she won't wish us to give up everything. Let's each buy what we want, and have a little fun. I'm sure we work hard enough to earn it," cried Jo, examining the heels of her shoes like a grown-up.

"I know *I* do—teaching those tiresome children nearly all day, when I'm longing to enjoy myself at home," Meg complained.

"You don't have half such a hard time as I do," said Jo. "How would you like to be shut up for hours with a nervous, fussy old lady, who keeps you trotting, is never satisfied, and worries you till you're ready to fly out of the window or cry!"

"It's naughty to fret, but I do think washing dishes and keeping things tidy is the worst work in the world. It makes me cross, and my hands get so stiff, I can't practice well at all." And Beth looked at her rough hands with a sigh that everyone could hear.

"I don't believe any of you suffer as I do," cried Amy, "for you don't have to go to school with insolent girls, who plague you if you don't know your lessons, and laugh at your dresses, and label your father if he isn't rich, and insult you when your nose isn't nice."

"If you mean *libel*, I'd say so, and not talk about *labels*, as if Papa was a pickle jar," advised Jo, laughing.

"I know what I mean, and you needn't be so *statirical* about it. It's proper to use good words, and improve your *vocabilary*," returned Amy, with dignity.

"Don't peck at one another, children. Don't you wish we had the money Papa lost when we were little, Jo? Dear me! How happy and good we'd be, if we had no worries!" said Meg, who could remember better times.

"You said the other day you thought we were much happier than the King children, for they were fighting and fretting all the time, in spite of their money."

"So I did, Beth. Well, I think we are. Though we do have to work, we make fun for ourselves, and are a pretty jolly set, as Jo would say."

"Jo does use such slang words!" observed Amy, with a reproving look at Jo's long figure stretched on the rug. Jo immediately sat up, put her hands in her pockets, and began to whistle.

"Don't, Jo, it's so boyish!"

"That's why I do it."

"I detest rude, unladylike girls!"

"I hate put-on, namby-pamby prissies!"

"Birds in their little nests agree," sang Beth, the peace-maker, with such a funny face that both sharp voices softened to a laugh, and the "pecking" ended for that time.

"Really, girls, you are both to blame," said Meg, beginning to lecture in her elder-sisterly fashion. "You are old enough to leave off boyish tricks, and to behave better, Josephine. It didn't matter so much when you were a little girl. But now you are so tall, and wear your hair up in a net, you should remember that you are a young lady."

"I'm not! And if my hair-do makes me one, I'll wear it in pigtails till I'm twenty," cried Jo, pulling off her net, and shaking down her chestnut-brown hair. "I hate to think I have to grow up, and be Miss March, and wear long gowns, and look prim! It's bad enough to be a girl, any-way, when I like boys' games and work and manners! I can't get over my disappointment in not being a boy. It's worse than ever now, for I'm dying to go and fight with Papa, and I can only stay at home and knit, like a poky old woman!" And Jo shook the blue army sock till the knitting needles rattled like castanets, and her ball of yarn bounded across the room.

"Poor Jo! It's too bad, but it can't be helped. So you must try to be contented with making your name boyish, and playing brother to us girls," said Beth, stroking Jo's head with a hand that all the dishwashing and dusting in the world could not make ungentle in its touch.

"As for you, Amy," continued Meg, "you are altogether too particular and prim. Your airs are funny now, but you'll grow up a pretentious little goose, if you don't take care. I like your nice manners and refined ways of speaking, when you don't try to be elegant. But your absurd words are as bad as Jo's slang."

"If Jo is a tomboy and Amy a goose, what am I, please?" asked Beth, ready to share the lecture.

"You're a dear, and nothing else," answered Meg warmly. No one contradicted her, for the "Mouse" was the pet of the family.

The four sisters sat knitting away in the twilight, while the December snow fell quietly without, and the fire crackled cheerfully within. It was a comfortable old room, though the carpet was faded and the furniture plain, for a good picture or two hung on the walls, books filled the recesses, chrysanthemums and Christmas roses bloomed in the windows, and a pleasant atmosphere of home peace pervaded it.

Margaret, the eldest of the four, was sixteen, and very pretty, being plump and fair, with large eyes, plenty of soft, brown hair, a sweet mouth, and white hands, of which she was rather vain. Fifteen-year-old Jo was tall, thin, and brown, and reminded one of a colt, for she never seemed to know what to do with her long limbs, which were very much in her way. She had a decided mouth, a comical nose, and sharp, gray eyes, which appeared to see everything, and were by turns fierce, funny, or thoughtful. Her long, thick hair was her one beauty, but it was usually bundled into a net, to be out of her way. Elizabeth or Beth, as everyone called her, was a rosy, smooth-haired, bright-eyed girl of thirteen, with a shy manner, a timid voice, and a peaceful expression which was seldom disturbed. Her father called her "Little Tranquility," and the name suited her excellently, for she seemed to live in a happy world of her own, only venturing out to meet the few whom she trusted and loved. Amy, though the youngest, was a most important person—in her own opinion, at least. A regular snow maiden, with blue eyes, and yellow hair curling on her shoulders, pale and slender, and always carrying herself like a young lady mindful of her manners.

The clock struck six and, having swept up the hearth, Beth put a pair of slippers down to warm. Somehow the sight of the old slippers had a good effect upon the girls, for Mother was coming, and everyone brightened to welcome her. Meg stopped lecturing and lighted the lamp, Amy got out of the easy chair without being asked, and Jo forgot how tired she was as she sat up to hold the slippers nearer to the blaze.

"They are quite worn out. Marmee must have a new pair."

"I thought I'd get her some with my dollar," said Beth.

"No, I shall!" cried Amy.

"I'm the oldest," began Meg, but Jo cut in—"I'm the man of the family now that Papa is away, and *I* shall provide the slippers, for he told me to take special care of Mother while he was gone."

"I'll tell you what we'll do," said Beth, "let's each get her something for Christmas, and not get anything for ourselves."

"That's like you, dear! What will we get!" exclaimed Jo.

Everyone thought soberly for a minute, then Meg announced, as if the idea was suggested by the sight of her own pretty hands, "I shall give her a nice pair of gloves."

"Army slippers, best to be had," cried Jo.

"Some handkerchiefs, all hemmed," said Beth.

"I'll get a little bottle of cologne. She likes it, and it won't cost much, so I'll have some left to buy my pencils," added Amy.

"Let Marmee think we are getting things for ourselves, and then surprise her. We must go shopping tomorrow afternoon, Meg. There is still so much to do about the new play for Christmas night," said Jo, marching up and down, with her hands behind her back and her nose in the air.

Then the girls rehearsed their original new play, which included a beautiful girl named Zara, a witch with a kettle full of simmering toads, a handsome hero named Roderigo, and a villain who died of arsenic poisoning.

"It's the best we've had yet," said Meg, as the dead villain sat up and rubbed his elbows.

"I don't see how you can write and act such splendid things, Jo. You're a regular Shakespeare!" exclaimed Beth.

"Not quite," replied Jo modestly. She rolled her eyes and struck a tragic pose, and the rehearsal ended in laughter.

"Glad to find you so merry, my girls," said a cheery voice at the door, and actors and audience turned to welcome a tall, motherly lady with a "can-I-help-you" look about her which was truly delightful. She was not elegantly dressed, but a noble-looking woman, and the girls thought the gray cloak and unfashionable bonnet covered the most splendid mother in the world.

"Well, dearies, how have you got on today? There was so much to do, getting the boxes ready to go tomorrow, that I didn't come home to lunch. Has anyone called, Beth? How is your cold, Meg? Jo, you look tired to death. Come and kiss me, baby."

Mrs. March got her wet things off, her warm slippers on, and sitting down in the easy chair, drew Amy to her lap, preparing to enjoy the happiest hour of her busy day. The girls flew about, trying to make things comfortable, each in her own way. Meg arranged the tea table, Jo brought wood and set chairs, dropping, overturning, and clattering everything she touched, Beth trotted to and fro between parlor and kitchen, quiet and busy, while Amy gave directions to everyone, as she sat with her hands folded.

As they gathered about the table, Mrs. March said, with a particularly happy face, "I've got a treat for you after supper."

A quick, bright smile went round like a streak of sunshine. Beth clapped her hands, regardless of the biscuit she held, and Jo tossed up her napkin, crying, "A letter! A letter! Three cheers for Father! "

"Yes, a nice long letter. He is well, and thinks he shall get through the cold season better than we feared. He sends all sorts of loving wishes for Christmas, and a special message to you girls," said Mrs. March, patting her pocket as if she had a treasure there.

"Hurry and get done! Don't stop to quirk your little finger and simper over your plate, Amy," cried Jo, choking on her tea and dropping her bread, butter side down, on the carpet in her haste to get at the treat.

Beth ate no more, but crept away to sit in her shadowy corner and brood over the delight to come, till the others were ready.

"I think it was so splendid of Father to go as a chaplain when he was too old to be drafted, and not strong enough to be a soldier," said Meg.

"Don't I wish I could go as a drummer or a nurse, so I could be near him and help him," exclaimed Jo.

"It must be very disagreeable to sleep in a tent, and eat all sorts of bad-tasting things, and drink out of a tin mug," sighed Amy.

"When will he come home, Marmee?" asked Beth, with a little quiver in her voice.

"Not for many months, dear, unless he is sick. He will stay and do his work faithfully as long as he can, and we won't ask for him back a minute sooner than he can be spared. Now come and hear the letter."

They all drew to the fire, Mother in the big chair with Beth at her feet, Meg and Amy perched on either arm of the chair, and Jo leaning on the back. The letter said little of the hardships endured, the dangers faced, or the home-sickness conquered. It was a cheerful, hopeful letter, full of lively descriptions of camp life, marches, and military news, and only at the end did the writer's heart overflow with fatherly love and longing for the little girls at home.

"Give them all my dear love and a kiss. Tell them I think of them by day, and pray for them by night. A year seems very long to wait before I see them, but remind them that while we wait we may all work, so that these hard days need not be wasted. I know they will remember all I said to them, that they will be loving children to you, will do their duty faithfully, fight their enemies bravely, and develop so beautifully that when I come back to them I may be fonder and prouder than ever of my little women."

Everybody sniffed when they came to that part. Jo wasn't ashamed of the great tear that dropped off the end of her nose, and Amy never minded the rumpling of her curls as she hid her face on her mother's shoulder and sobbed out, "I am a selfish girl! But I'll truly try to be better, so he won't be disappointed in me."

"We all will!" cried Meg. "I think too much of my looks and hate to work, but I won't any more, if I can help it."

"I'll try and be what he loves to call me, 'a little woman,' and not be rough and wild, but do my duty here instead of wanting to be somewhere else," said Jo, thinking that keeping her temper at home was a much harder task than facing enemies on a battlefield.

Beth said nothing, but wiped away her tears with the blue army sock and began to knit with all her might, losing no time in doing the duty that lay nearest her, while she resolved in her quiet little soul to be all that Father hoped to find her when the year brought round the happy coming home.

Mrs. March broke the silence that followed Jo's words, by saying in her cheery voice, "Do you remember how you used to play the Pilgrim's Progress story when you were little? I let you travel through the house from the cellar, which was the City of Destruction, up, up, to the housetop, where you had all the lovely things you could collect to make a Celestial City."

"What fun it was, especially going by the lions, fighting and passing through the valley where the hobgoblins were!" said Jo.

"I liked the place where our heavy burdens tumbled downstairs," said Meg.

"My favorite part was when we came out on the flat roof where our flowers and arbors and pretty things were, and all stood and sang for joy up there in the sunshine," said Beth, smiling as if that pleasant moment had come back.

"I don't remember much about it, except that I was afraid of the cellar and the dark entry, and always liked the cake and milk we had up at the top. If I wasn't too old for such things, I'd rather like to play it over again," said Amy, at the mature age of twelve.

"We never are too old for this, my dear, because it is a play we are playing all the time in one way or another. Our burdens are here, our road is before us, and the longing for goodness and happiness is the guide that leads us through many troubles and mistakes to the peace which is a true Celestial City. Now, my little pilgrims, suppose you begin again, not in play, but in earnest, and see how far on you can get before Father comes home."

"Let us do it," said Meg thoughtfully. "It is only another name for trying to be good, and the story may help us. Though we do want to be good, it's hard work and we forget, and don't do our best."

"We ought to have directions, like Christian in the story. What shall we do about that?" asked Jo, delighted with a fantasy which lent a little romance to the dull task of doing her duty.

"Look under your pillows Christmas morning, and you will find your guidebook," replied Mrs. March.

They talked over the new plan, then out came the four little workbaskets, and the needles flew as the girls made sheets for Aunt March. It was uninteresting sewing, but tonight no one grumbled. They adopted Jo's plan of dividing the long seams into four parts, and calling the quarters Europe, Asia, Africa, and America, and in that way got on fine, especially when they talked about the different countries as they stitched their way through them.

At 9:00 they stopped work, and sang, as usual, before they went to bed. No one but Beth could get much music out of the old piano, but she had a way of softly touching the yellow keys and making a pleasant accompaniment. Meg had a voice like a flute, and she and her mother led the little choir. Amy chirped like a cricket, and Jo wandered through the airs at her own sweet will, always coming out at the wrong place. They had always sung together from the time they could lisp "Crinkle, crinkle, 'ittle 'tar."

2

A MERRY CHRISTMAS

Jo WAS THE FIRST TO WAKE in the gray dawn of Christmas morning. No stockings were hung at the fireplace, and for a moment she felt as much disappointed as she did once long ago, when her little sock fell down because it was so crammed with goodies. Then she remembered her mother's promise and, slipping her hand under her pillow, drew out a little crimson-covered book. She knew it well, for it was that beautiful old story of the best life ever lived, and Jo felt that it was a true guidebook for any pilgrim going on life's long journey.

She woke Meg with a "Merry Christmas," and told her to see what was under her pillow. A green-covered book appeared, with the same picture inside, and a few words written by their mother, which made their one present precious in their eyes. Presently Beth and Amy woke to rummage and find their little books also—one dove-colored, the other blue—and all sat looking at and talking about them, while the east grew rosy with the coming day.

In spite of her little faults, Margaret had a sweet nature, which influenced her sisters, especially Jo, who loved her tenderly, and obeyed her because her advice was so gently given.

"Girls," said Meg seriously, looking from Jo's tumbled head beside her to the two little nightcapped girls in the room beyond, "you can do as you please, but I shall keep my book on the table here and read a little every morning as soon as I wake, for I know it will do me good and help me through the day."

Then she opened her New Testament and began to read. Jo put her arm round her and, leaning cheek to cheek, read also, with the quiet expression so seldom seen on her restless face.

"How good Meg is! Come, Amy, let's do as they do. I'll help you with the hard words, and they'll explain things if we don't understand," whispered Beth, very much impressed by the pretty books and her sisters' example.

"I'm glad mine is blue," said Amy. And then the rooms were still while the pages were softly turned, and the winter sunshine crept in to touch the bright heads and serious faces with a Christmas greeting.

"Where is Mother?" asked Meg, as she and Jo ran down to thank her for their gifts, half an hour later.

"Goodness only knows. Some poor critter come a-beggin', and your ma went straight off to see what was needed. There never was such a woman for giving away vittles and drink, clothes and firewood," replied Hannah, who had lived with the family since Meg was born, and was considered more as a friend than hired help.

"She will be back soon, I think, so fry your cakes, and have everything ready," said Meg, looking over the presents which were collected in a basket and kept under the sofa, ready to be produced at the proper time. "Why, where is Amy's bottle of cologne?" she added, as the little flask did not appear.

"She took it out a minute ago, and went off with it to put a ribbon on it, or some such notion," replied Jo, dancing about the room to take the first stiffness off the new army slippers.

"How nice my handkerchiefs look, don't they? Hannah washed and ironed them for me, and I marked them all myself," said Beth, looking proudly at the somewhat uneven letters which had cost her such labor.

"Bless the child! She's gone and put 'Mother' on them instead of 'M.

"She will be back soon, I think . . . so have everything ready," said Meg,
looking over the presents which were collected in a basket.

March.' How funny!" cried Jo, taking up one.

"Isn't it right? I thought it was better to do it so, because Meg's initials are M. M., and I don't want anyone to use these but Marmee," said Beth, looking troubled.

"It's all right, dear, and a very pretty idea—quite sensible, too, for no one can ever mistake now. It will please her very much, I know," said Meg, with a frown for Jo and a smile for Beth.

"There's Mother. Hide the basket, quick!" cried Jo, as a door slammed and steps sounded in the hall.

Amy came in hastily, and looked abashed when she saw her sisters all waiting for her.

"Where have you been, and what are you hiding behind you?" asked Meg, surprised to see, by her hood and cloak, that lazy Amy had been out so early.

"Don't laugh at me, Jo! I didn't mean anyone should know till the time came. I only meant to change the little bottle for a big one, and I gave *all* my money to get it, and I'm truly trying not to be selfish any more."

As she spoke, Amy showed the handsome flask which replaced the cheap one, and looked so earnest and humble in her little effort to forget herself that Meg hugged her on the spot, and Jo pronounced her "a trump," while Beth ran to the window, and picked her finest rose to ornament the stately bottle.

"You see I felt ashamed of my present, after reading and talking about being good this morning, so I ran round the corner and changed it the minute I was up: and I'm so glad, for mine is the handsomest now."

Another bang of the street door sent the basket under the sofa, and the girls to the table, eager for breakfast.

"Merry Christmas, Marmee! Many of them! Thank you for our books. We read some, and mean to every day," they cried, in chorus.

"Merry Christmas, little daughters! I'm glad you began at once, and

20

hope you will keep on. But I want to say one word before we sit down. Not far away from here lies a poor woman with a little newborn baby. Six children are huddled into one bed to keep from freezing, for they have no fire. There is nothing to eat over there, and the oldest boy came to tell me they were suffering hunger and cold. My girls, will you give them your breakfast as a Christmas present?"

They were all unusually hungry, having waited nearly an hour, and for a minute no one spoke—only a minute, for Jo exclaimed, "I'm so glad you came before we began!"

"May I go and help carry the things to the poor little children?" asked Beth eagerly.

"I shall take the cream and the muffins," added Amy, heroically giving up the articles she most liked.

Meg was already covering the buckwheats, and piling the bread into one big plate.

"I thought you'd do it," said Mrs. March, smiling as if satisfied. "You shall all go and help me, and when we come back we will have bread and milk for breakfast, and make it up at dinnertime."

They were soon ready, and the procession set out. Fortunately it was early, and they went through back streets, so few people saw them, and no one laughed at the queer party.

A poor, bare, miserable room it was, with broken windows, no fire, ragged bedclothes, a sick mother, wailing baby, and a group of pale, hungry children cuddled under one old quilt, trying to keep warm.

How the big eyes stared and the blue lips smiled as the girls went in!

"*Ach, mein Gott!* It is good angels come to us!" said the poor woman, crying for joy.

"Funny angels in hoods and mittens," said Jo, and set them laughing.

In a few minutes it did seem as if kind spirits had been at work there. Hannah, who had carried wood, made a fire, and stopped up the broken panes with old hats and her own cloak. Mrs. March gave the mother tea and gruel, and comforted her with promises of help, while she dressed the little baby as tenderly as if it had been her own. The girls meantime spread the table, set the children round the fire, and fed them like so many hungry birds—laughing, talking, and trying to understand their funny broken English.

"*Das ist gut! Die Engel-kinder!*" cried the poor things as they ate and warmed their purple hands at the comfortable blaze.

The girls had never been called angel children before, and thought it agreeable. That was a happy breakfast, though they didn't get any of it. And when they went away, leaving comfort behind, there were not in all the city four merrier people than the hungry little girls who gave away their breakfasts and contented themselves with bread and milk on Christmas morning.

"That's loving our neighbor better than ourselves, and I like it," said Meg, as they set out their presents while their mother was upstairs collecting clothes for the poor Hummel children.

There was a great deal of love done up in the few little bundles. The tall vase of red roses, white chrysanthemums, and trailing vines, which stood in the middle, gave an elegant air to the table.

"She's coming! Strike up the piano, Beth! Open the door, Amy! Three cheers for Marmee!" cried Jo, prancing about while Meg went to conduct Mother to the seat of honor.

Beth played her gayest march, Amy threw open the door, and Meg brought in their mother. She smiled with her eyes full as she examined her presents and read the little notes which accompanied them. The slippers went on at once, a new handkerchief was slipped into her pocket, well scented with Amy's cologne, the rose was fastened in her bosom, and the nice gloves were pronounced a "perfect fit."

There was a good deal of laughing and kissing and explaining, in the simple, loving fashion which makes family celebrations so pleasant at the time and so sweet to remember long afterward.

The rest of the day was devoted to preparations for the evening festivities. The girls put their wits to work, and—necessity being the mother of invention—made whatever props they needed, such as a cardboard guitar. Jo had a pair of leather boots, an old sword, and a slashed doublet that she used in all her plays. Each of the girls took several parts apiece, whisking in and out of various costumes, and managing the stage besides.

On Christmas night, a dozen neighborhood girls piled onto a folding cot and sat before the blue and yellow chintz curtains in a most flattering state of expectancy. There was a good deal of rustling and whispering behind the curtain, and an occasional giggle from Amy, who tended to get hysterical during all the excitement. Presently a bell sounded, the curtains flew apart, and Jo's *Operatic Tragedy* began. By the time the play was over and the hero had won beautiful Zara, there had been five acts plus an intermission with candy for all the audience.

Tumultuous applause followed but was cut short—for the folding cot on which the audience sat suddenly folded up. The hero and Zara's father flew to the rescue, and all were taken out unhurt, though many were speechless with laughter. The excitement had hardly subsided when Hannah appeared, with "Mrs. March's compliments, and would the ladies walk down to refreshments."

This was a surprise even to the actors, and when they saw the table, they looked at one another in rapturous amazement. It was like Marmee to get up a little treat for them, but anything so fine as this was unheard of since the departed days of plenty. There was ice cream—actually two dishes of it, pink and white—and cake and fruit and distracting French bonbons and, in the middle of the table, four great bouquets of hothouse flowers!

It took their breath away. They stared first at the table and then at their mother, who looked as if she enjoyed it immensely.

"Is it fairies?" asked Amy.

"It's Santa Claus," said Beth.

"Mother did it." And Meg smiled her sweetest, in spite of the gray beard and white eyebrows she was still wearing.

"Aunt March had a good fit and sent the treats," cried Jo, with a sudden inspiration.

"All wrong. Old Mr. Laurence sent it," replied Mrs. March.

"The Laurence boy's grandfather! What in the world put such a thing into his head? We don't know him!" exclaimed Meg.

"Hannah told one of his servants about your breakfast party. He is an odd old gentleman, but that pleased him. He knew my father years ago, and he sent me a polite note this afternoon, saying he hoped I would allow him to express his friendly feeling toward my children by sending them a few trifles in honor of the day. I could not refuse, and so you have a little feast at night to make up for the bread-and-milk breakfast."

"That boy put it into his head, I know he did! He's a capital fellow, and I wish we could get acquainted. He looks as if he'd like to know us but he's bashful, and Meg is so prim she won't let me speak to him when we pass," said Jo, as the plates went round, and the ice cream began to melt out of sight, with ohs and ahs of satisfaction.

"You mean the people who live in the big house next door, don't you?" asked one of the girls. "My mother knows old Mr. Laurence, but says he's proud and doesn't like to mix with his neighbors. He keeps his grandson shut up, when he isn't riding or walking with his tutor, and makes him study very hard. We invited the grandson to our party, but he didn't come. Mother says he's very nice, though he never speaks to us girls."

"Our cat ran away once, and he brought her back, and we talked over the fence, and were getting on fine—all about cricket, and so on—when he saw Meg coming and walked off. I mean to know him someday, for he needs fun, I'm sure he does," said Jo decidedly.

"I like his manners, and he looks like a little gentleman," said Mrs. March. "He brought the flowers himself, and I should have asked him in, if I had been sure what was going on upstairs. He looked so wistful as he went away, hearing the frolic and evidently having none of his own."

"It's a mercy you didn't, Mother!" laughed Jo, looking at her boots. "But we'll have another play sometime that he can see. Perhaps he'll help act. Wouldn't that be jolly?"

"I never had such a fine bouquet before! How pretty it is!" And Meg examined her flowers with great interest.

"They *are* lovely! But Beth's roses are sweeter to me," said Mrs. March, smelling the half-dead posy in her belt.

Beth nestled up to her, and whispered softly, "I wish I could send my bunch to Father. I'm afraid he isn't having such a merry Christmas as we are."

3
THE LAURENCE BOY

"Jo! Jo! Where are you?" cried Meg at the foot of the garret stairs.

"Here!" answered a husky voice from above. Running up, Meg found her sister eating apples and crying over a romantic novel, wrapped up in a comforter on an old three-legged sofa by the sunny window. This was Jo's favorite refuge, which she shared with a pet rat who lived near by and didn't mind her a particle. As Meg appeared, Scrabble whisked into his hole. Jo shook the tears off her cheeks and waited to hear the news.

"Such fun! Only see! A regular invitation from Mrs. Gardiner for tomorrow night!" cried Meg, waving the precious paper and then proceeding to read it with girlish delight.

" 'Mrs. Gardiner would be happy to see Miss March and Miss Josephine at a little dance on New Year's Eve.' Marmee is willing we should go, now what *shall* we wear?"

"What's the use of asking that, when you know we shall wear our poplins, because we haven't got anything else?" answered Jo with her mouth full.

"If I only had a silk!" sighed Meg. "Mother says I may when I'm eighteen perhaps, but two years is an everlasting time to wait."

"I'm sure our poplins look like silk, and they are nice enough for us.

Yours is as good as new, but I forgot the burn and the tear in mine. Whatever shall I do? The burn shows badly."

"You must sit still all you can and keep your back out of sight. The front is all right. I shall have a new ribbon for my hair, and Marmee will lend me her little pearl pin, and my new slippers are lovely, and my gloves will do, though they aren't as nice as I'd like."

"My gloves are spoiled with lemonade, and I can't get any new ones, so I shall have to go without," said Jo, who never troubled herself much about clothes.

"You *must* have gloves, or I won't go," cried Meg decidedly. "Gloves are more important than anything else. You shouldn't dance without them, and if you do I should be so mortified."

"Then I'll stay still."

"You can't ask Mother for new ones, they are so expensive, and you are so careless. She said when you spoiled the others that she shouldn't get you any more this winter. Can't you make them do?" asked Meg anxiously.

"I can hold them crumpled up in my hand, so no one will know how stained they are. That's all I can do. No! I'll tell you how we can manage—each wear one good glove and carry a bad one. Don't you see?"

"Your hands are bigger than mine, and you will stretch my glove dreadfully," began Meg, whose gloves were a tender point with her.

"Then I'll go without. I don't care what people say!" cried Jo, taking up her book.

"You may have it, you may! Only don't stain it, and do behave nicely. Don't put your hands behind you, or stare, or say 'Christopher Columbus!' will you?"

"Don't worry about me. I'll be as prim as I can and not get into any scrapes, if I can help it. Now go and answer the invitation, and let me finish this splendid story."

So Meg went away to prepare for the party, while Jo finished her story, her four apples, and a game of romps with Scrabble.

On New Year's Eve the two younger girls helped the two elder with the all-important business of "getting ready for the party." There was a great deal of running up and down, laughing and talking. Meg wanted a few curls about her face, and Jo undertook to wrap some wet strands of hair in paper and wind them into curls with a pair of hot tongs.

"Ought they to smoke like that?" asked Beth from her perch on the bed.

"It's the dampness drying," replied Jo.

"What a queer smell! It's like burned feathers," observed Amy, smoothing her own pretty curls with a superior air.

"There, now I'll take off the papers and you'll see a cloud of little ringlets," said Jo, putting down the tongs.

She did take off the papers, but no cloud of ringlets appeared, for the hair came with the papers, and the horrified hairdresser laid a row of little scorched bundles on the bureau before her victim.

"Oh, oh, oh! What *have* you done! I'm spoiled! I can't go! My hair, oh, my hair!" wailed Meg, looking with despair at the uneven frizzle on her forehead.

"Just my luck! You shouldn't have asked me to do it. I always spoil everything. I'm so sorry, but the tongs were too hot, and so I've made a mess," groaned poor Jo, with tears of regret.

"It isn't spoiled. Just frizzle it, and tie your ribbons so the ends come on your forehead a bit, and it will look like the latest fashion. I've seen many girls do it so," said Amy consolingly.

"Serves me right for trying to be fine. I wish I'd let my hair alone," cried Meg.

"So do I, it was so smooth and pretty. But it will soon grow out," said Beth, coming to kiss and comfort the shorn sheep.

Meg was in silvery gray, with a blue velvet snood, lace frills, and the pearl pin. Jo in maroon, with a stiff linen collar and a white chrysanthemum for her only ornament. Each put on one nice glove, and carried one soiled one. Meg's high-heeled slippers were too tight and hurt her, though she would not admit it, and Jo's nineteen hairpins all seemed stuck straight into her head, which was not exactly comfortable—but, dear me, let us be elegant or die!

"Have a good time, dearies!" said Mrs. March, as the sisters went daintily down the walk. "Don't eat much, and come away at 11:00 when I send Hannah for you." As the gate clashed behind them, a voice cried from a window, "Girls, girls! Have you both got nice pocket handkerchiefs?"

"Yes, yes, and Meg has cologne on hers," cried Jo, adding with a laugh as they went on, "I do believe Marmee would ask that if we were all running away from an earthquake."

"It is one of her aristocratic tastes, and quite proper, for a real lady is always known by neat boots, gloves, and handkerchief," replied Meg, who had a good many little "aristocratic tastes" of her own.

"If you see me doing anything wrong, just remind me by a wink, will you?" asked Jo, giving her collar a twitch and her head a hasty brush.

"No, winking isn't ladylike. I'll lift my eyebrows if anything is wrong, and nod if you are all right. Now hold your shoulders straight, and take short steps, and don't shake hands if you are introduced to anyone: it isn't in style."

"How do you learn all the proper ways? I never can. Isn't that music gay?"

At the party, Jo felt as much out of place as a colt in a flower garden. No one came to talk to her, and one by one the group near her dwindled away till she was left alone. When the dancing began Meg was asked at once, and Jo slipped into a tiny side-room, intending to peep out and enjoy herself in peace. Unfortunately, another bashful person had chosen the same refuge, and she found herself face to face with the "Laurence boy."

"Dear me, I didn't know anyone was here!" stammered Jo, preparing to back out as speedily as she had bounced in. But he asked her to stay.

"How is your cat, Miss March?" asked the boy, trying to look sober while his black eyes shone with fun.

"Nicely, thank you, Mr. Laurence. But I am not Miss March, I'm only Jo," returned the young lady.

"I'm not Mr. Laurence, I'm only Laurie."

"Laurie Laurence—what an odd name!"

"My first name is Theodore, but I don't like it, for the fellows called me Dora, so I made them say Laurie instead."

"I hate my name, too—so sentimental! I wish every one would say Jo instead of Josephine. How did you make the boys stop calling you Dora?"

"I thrashed 'em."

Jo's eager questions soon set Laurie going, and he told her how he had been at school in Switzerland, where the boys had a fleet of boats on the lake, and for holiday fun went on walking trips with their teachers.

"Don't I wish I'd been there!" cried Jo. "Did you go to Paris?"

"We spent last winter there."

"Can you talk French?"

"We were not allowed to speak anything else."

"Do say some! I can read it, but can't pronounce."

Jo soon liked the "Laurence boy" better than ever and took several good looks at him, so that she might describe him to her sisters, for they had few male cousins, and boys were almost unknown creatures to them.

"Curly black hair, brown skin, big black eyes, handsome nose, taller than I am, very polite for a boy, and altogether jolly. I wonder how old he is?" she thought.

It was on the tip of Jo's tongue to ask, but she checked herself in time and, with unusual tact, tried to find out in a roundabout way.

"I suppose you are going to college soon?"

"Not for a year or two. I won't go before seventeen, anyway."

"Are you only fifteen?" asked Jo, looking at the tall lad, whom she had imagined seventeen already.

"Sixteen, next month."

"How I wish I was going to college! Listen to that splendid polka! Why don't you go and try it?"

"If you will come too," he answered, with a gallant little bow.

That is why Jo decided to explain to Laurie about the scorch on the back of her dress, which came from standing too close to the fireplace. She thought that Laurie would laugh at her, but he didn't.

He said gently, "Never mind that. I'll tell you how we can manage. There's a long hall out there, and we can dance grandly, and no one will see us. Please come."

The hall was empty, and they had a grand polka, for Laurie danced well, and taught her the German step, which delighted Jo, being full of swing and spring. When the music stopped, they sat down on the stairs to get their breath, and Laurie was in the midst of an account of a students' festival at Heidelberg when Meg appeared in a doorway and beckoned. Jo reluctantly followed her into a side room, where she found her on a sofa, holding her foot, and looking pale.

"I've sprained my ankle. That stupid high heel turned and gave me a sad wrench. It aches so, I can hardly stand, and I don't know how I'm ever going to get home," she said, rocking to and fro in pain.

"I'll go out and try to find someone to get us a carriage from the stable," said Jo.

"No, indeed! It's past 9:00, and dark as Egypt. I'll rest till Hannah comes for us, and then do the best I can. I can't dance any more, but as soon as dessert is over, watch for Hannah and tell me the minute she comes."

"They are going to have dessert now. I'll stay with you. I'd rather."

"No, dear, run along, and bring me some coffee. I'm so tired!"

So Meg reclined, and Jo went blundering away to the dining room. Making a dart at the table, she secured the coffee, which she immediately spilled, thereby making the front of her dress as bad as the back.

"Oh, dear, what a blunderbuss I am!" exclaimed Jo, finishing Meg's glove by scrubbing her gown with it.

"Can I help you?" said a friendly voice. And there was Laurie, with a full cup in one hand and a plate of ice cream in the other.

"I was trying to get something for Meg, who is very tired, and some-one shook me, and here I am in a nice state," answered Jo, glancing dismally from the stained skirt to the coffee-colored glove.

"Too bad! I was looking for someone to give this to. May I take it to your sister?"

"Oh, thank you! I'll show you where she is. I don't offer to take it myself, for I should only get into another scrape if I did."

Jo led the way, and Laurie drew up a little table, brought a second installment of coffee and ice cream for Jo, and was so obliging that even particular Meg pronounced him a "nice boy." They were having a merry time with some other young people who had strayed in, when Hannah appeared. Meg forgot her foot and rose so quickly that she was forced to catch hold of Jo, with an exclamation of pain.

"Hush! Don't say anything," she whispered, adding aloud, "It's noth-ing. I turned my foot a little, that's all," and limped upstairs to put her things on.

Jo ran downstairs and asked a servant if he could get her a carriage. He couldn't, but Laurie overheard what she said and offered his grandfather's carriage, which had just come for him.

"Please let me take you home. It's on my way, you know, and it's rain-ing."

That settled it. Telling him of Meg's mishap, Jo gratefully accepted and rushed up to bring down Meg and Hannah. Hannah hated rain as much as a cat does, so she made no trouble. They rolled away in the luxurious carriage feeling festive and elegant. Laurie rode with the driver so Meg could keep her foot up, and the girls talked over their party.

"I had a capital time. Did you?" asked Jo, rumpling up her hair, and making herself comfortable.

Meg said that she had a new friend named Annie Moffat who invited her to come and spend a week in the spring and attend an opera, if Mother would give permission. And she had danced with a polite young man with auburn hair.

"He looked like a grasshopper in a fit when he did the new dance step. Laurie and I couldn't help laughing. Did you hear us?"

"No, but it was very rude. What *were* you about all that time, hidden away there?"

Jo told her adventures, and by the time she had finished they were at home. With many thanks, they said good night and crept in, hoping to disturb no one. But the instant their door creaked, two little nightcaps bobbed up, and two sleepy but eager voices cried out, "Tell about the party! Tell about the party!"

Jo had saved some bonbons for the little girls, and they soon subsided after hearing the most thrilling events of the evening.

"I declare, it really seems like being a fine young lady, to come home from the party in a carriage and sit in my dressing gown with a maid to wait on me," said Meg, as Jo bound up her foot and brushed her hair.

"I don't believe fine young ladies enjoy themselves a bit more than we do, in spite of our burned hair, old gowns, one glove apiece, and tight slippers that sprain our ankles when we are silly enough to wear them." And Jo was quite right.

4
BURDENS

"Oh, dear, how hard it is to pick up our burdens and go on," Meg sighed the morning after the party. Now that the holidays were over, the week of merrymaking had not made it easy to go back to a job she disliked.

"I wish it was Christmas or New Year's all the time. Wouldn't it be fun?" answered Jo, yawning dismally. "Well, we can't have it, so don't let us grumble but shoulder our bundles and trudge along as cheerfully as Marmee does. Aunt March is a heavy burden to me, but I suppose when I've learned to carry her without complaining, she will tumble off, or get so light that I shan't mind her."

Jo's idea put her in good spirits, but Meg didn't brighten, for her burden, consisting of four spoiled children, seemed heavier than ever. She put back the ribbon she was going to tie around her neck.

"What's the use of looking nice, when no one sees me but those cross midgets, and no one cares whether I'm pretty or not!" she muttered, shutting her drawer with a jerk. "I shall have to toil and moil all my days, with only little bits of fun now and then, and get old and ugly and sour, because I'm poor and can't enjoy my life as other girls do. It's a shame!"

So Meg went downstairs, wearing an injured look, and wasn't at all agreeable at breakfast time. Beth had a headache and lay on the sofa, trying to comfort herself with the cat and three kittens. Amy was fretting because her lessons were not learned, and she couldn't find her galoshes. Jo chose to whistle and make a great racket getting ready. Mrs. March was busy trying to finish a letter, which must go at once. Hannah had the grumps, for being up late at night didn't suit her.

"There never *was* such a cross family!" cried Jo, losing her temper when she had upset an inkstand, broken both boot lacings, and sat down upon her hat.

"You're the crossest person in it!" returned Amy, washing away her math that was all wrong with tears that had fallen on her slate.

"Beth, if you don't keep these horrid cats in the cellar I'll have them drowned," exclaimed Meg angrily, as she tried to get rid of the kitten which had scrambled up her back and stuck like a burr just out of reach.

Jo laughed, Meg scolded, Beth implored, and Amy wailed because she couldn't remember how much nine times twelve was.

"Girls, girls, do be quiet one minute! I *must* get this off by the early mail, and you drive me distracted with your fussing," cried Mrs. March, crossing out the third spoiled sentence in her letter.

There was a momentary lull, broken by Hannah, who stalked in, laid two hot turnovers on the table, and stalked out again. Meg and Jo called the turnovers "muffs," for they had no real muffs and found the hot pies comforting in their hands on cold mornings. Hannah never forgot to make them, no matter how busy or grumpy she might be, for the walk to work was long for the girls, and they got no other lunch.

"Cuddle your cats and get over your headache, Bethy. Good-bye, Marmee. We are a set of rascals this morning, but we'll come home regular angels. Come on, Meg!" And Jo tramped away, feeling that the pilgrims were not setting out as they ought to do.

They looked back before turning the corner, for their mother was always at the window to smile and wave her hand to them. Somehow it seemed as if they couldn't have got through the day without that, for the last glimpse of her motherly face was like sunshine.

"If Marmee shook her fist instead of kissing her hand to us, it would serve us right, for more ungrateful wretches were never seen," cried Jo, taking a remorseful satisfaction in the snowy walk and bitter wind.

"Don't use such dreadful expressions," said Meg from the depths of the scarf in which she had shrouded herself like a nun sick of the world.

"I like good strong words that mean something," replied Jo, catching her hat as it took a leap off her head before flying away altogether.

"Call yourself any names you like, but I am neither a rascal nor a wretch and I don't choose to be called so."

"Poor dear, just wait till I make my fortune, and you shall revel in carriages and ice cream and high-heeled slippers and posies and redheaded boys to dance with."

"How ridiculous you are, Jo!" But Meg laughed at the nonsense and felt better in spite of herself.

"Lucky for you I am, for if I put on crushed airs and tried to be dismal, as you do, we should be in a nice state. Thank goodness, I can always find something funny to keep me up."

Jo gave her sister an encouraging pat on the shoulder as they parted for the day, each hugging her little warm turnover, and each trying to be cheerful in spite of wintry weather and work.

When Mr. March had lost his property in trying to help an unfortunate friend, the two oldest girls begged to try to earn their own living. Their parents consented, and both went looking for jobs.

Margaret found a job as a child-care worker. She could remember when the March home was beautiful, life full of ease and pleasure. She tried not to be envious or discontented, but it was natural that she should long for pretty things and happy friends. At the Kings' she caught frequent glimpses of dainty ball dresses and bouquets, heard lively gossip about theaters, concerts, sleighing parties, and merrymakings of all kinds, and saw money lavished on trifles. Poor Meg seldom complained, but a sense of injustice made her feel bitter sometimes, for she had not yet learned how rich she was in the only blessings which can make life happy.

Jo happened to suit Aunt March, who was lame and needed someone to wait upon her. The childless old lady had offered to adopt one of the March girls when they became poor, and was much offended because her offer was declined. Other friends told the Marches that they had thus lost all chance of being remembered in the rich old lady's will, but they answered, "We can't give up our girls for a dozen fortunes. Rich or poor, we will keep together and be happy with one another."

The old lady wouldn't speak to them for a time, but when she happened to meet Jo at a friend's, something in Jo's comical face and blunt manners struck the old lady's fancy, and she offered to hire her. Jo accepted the job, since nothing better appeared, and to every one's surprise she got on remarkably well with her crotchety relative. There was an occasional tempest, and once Jo quit and went home. But Aunt March always sent for her with such urgency that she could not refuse, for in her heart she rather liked the peppery old lady.

Perhaps the real attraction for Jo was the large library of fine books which was left to dust and spiders since kind old Uncle March died. The moment Aunt March took her nap or was busy with company, Jo hurried to this wilderness of books, and curling herself up in the easy chair, devoured poetry, romance, history, travel, and pictures—like a regular bookworm. But, like all happiness, it did not last long, for as sure as she had just reached the heart of the story, a shrill voice called, "Josy-phine! Josy-phine!" and she had to leave her paradise to wind yarn, wash the poodle, or read Belsham's *Essays* to her aunt.

Jo's ambition was to do something splendid in life. A quick temper, sharp tongue, and restless spirit were always getting her into scrapes, and her life was a series of ups and downs which were both comic and pathetic. But the thought that she was doing something to support herself made her happy in spite of the perpetual "Josy-phine!"

Beth was too bashful to go to school, so she did her lessons at home with her father. Then he went away, and her mother went to work for the Soldiers' Aid Societies. She helped Hannah keep their home neat and comfortable, never thinking of any reward but to be loved. Her little world was peopled with imaginary friends, and she was by nature a busy bee. She set up a hospital for sick dolls. One forlorn fragment of *dollanity* had belonged to Jo and, having led a tempestuous life, was left a wreck in the rag bag, from which it was rescued by Beth and taken to her refuge. Because it had no top to its head, she tied on a neat little cap. And as both arms and legs were gone, she folded it in a blanket and devoted her best bed to this chronic invalid. If anyone had known the care lavished on that doll, it would have touched their hearts, even while they laughed. She sang it lullabies and never went to bed without kissing its dirty face and whispering tenderly, "I hope you'll have a good night, my poor dear."

Beth loved music so dearly, tried so hard to learn, and practiced away so patiently at the jingling old instrument, that it did seem as if someone like Aunt March ought to help her. Nobody did, however, and nobody saw Beth wipe the tears off the yellow keys, that wouldn't keep in tune, when she was all alone. Day after day she said hopefully to herself, "I know I'll get my music some time, if I'm good."

There are many Beths in the world, shy and quiet, living for others so cheerfully that no one sees the sacrifices till the little cricket on the hearth stops chirping, and the sweet, sunshiny presence vanishes, leaving silence and shadow behind.

If anybody had asked Amy what the greatest trial of her life was, she would have answered at once, "My nose." It was rather flat, and all the pinching in the world could not give it an aristocratic point. No one minded it but herself, and it was doing its best to grow, but Amy felt deeply her lack of a Grecian nose, and drew lots of handsome noses to console herself.

She was never so happy as when copying flowers, designing fairies, or illustrating stories. Her teachers complained that instead of doing her sums she covered her slate with animals, and ludicrous cartoons came fluttering out of all her books at unlucky moments. She got through her lessons as well as she could, and managed to be a model of behavior. Besides her drawing, she could play twelve tunes, crochet, and read French without mispronouncing more than two-thirds of the words. She had a plaintive way of saying, "When Papa was rich we did so-and-so," which was very touching, and her long words were considered "perfectly elegant" by the other girls.

Amy was becoming spoiled, and her small selfishnesses were growing nicely. One thing, however, quenched her pride: she had to wear her cousin Florence's outgrown clothes. Florence's mamma hadn't a particle of taste, and Amy suffered deeply at having to wear a red instead of a blue bonnet and unbecoming dresses. Everything was good, well made, and little worn, but Amy's artistic eyes were much afflicted, especially this winter, when her school dress was a dull purple with yellow dots and no trimming.

Meg and Jo meant a great deal to one another, but each took one of the younger girls into her keeping and watched over her. Meg was Amy's special friend, and by some strange attraction of opposites, Jo was gentle Beth's. Beth told her thoughts to no one except her big harum-scarum sister.

That evening as they sat sewing, Meg said, "Does anybody have anything to tell? It's been such a dismal day I'm dying for some amusement."

"I had a queer time with Aunt today, and, as I got the best of it, I'll tell you about it," began Jo, who dearly loved to tell stories. "I was reading that everlasting Belsham, and droning away as I always do, for Aunt soon dozes off, and then I take out some nice book, and read like fury till she wakes up. The minute her cap began to bob like a top-heavy dahlia, I whipped the *Vicar of Wakefield* out of my pocket, and read away, with one eye on him and one on Aunt. I'd just got to where they all tumbled into the water when I forgot and laughed out loud. Aunt woke up and, being more good-natured than usual after her nap, told me to read a bit and show what frivolous work I preferred to the worthy and instructive Belsham. I did my best, and she liked it, though she only said, 'I don't understand what it's all about. Go back and begin it, child.'

"Back I went, and made the Primrose family as interesting as ever I could. Once I was wicked enough to stop in a thrilling place, and say meekly, 'I'm afraid it tires you, ma'am. Shan't I stop now?'

"She caught up her knitting, which had dropped out of her hands, gave me a sharp look through her specs, and said, in her short way, 'Finish the chapter, and don't be impertinent, miss.' "

"Did she admit she liked it?" asked Meg.

"Oh, bless you, no! But she let old Belsham rest, and when I ran back after my gloves this afternoon, there she was, so absorbed in the Vicar that she didn't hear me laugh. What a pleasant life she might have if she only chose! I don't envy her much, in spite of her money."

"That reminds me," said Meg, "that I've got something to tell. At the Kings' today I found everybody in a flurry, and one of the children said that her oldest brother had done something dreadful, and Papa had sent him away. I heard Mrs. King crying and Mr. King talking very loud, and Grace and Ellen turned away their faces when they passed me, so I shouldn't see how red their eyes were. I didn't ask any questions, of course, but I felt so sorry for them and was glad I hadn't any wild brothers to do wicked things and disgrace the family."

"I think being disgraced in school is a great deal *tryinger* than anything bad boys can do," said Amy, shaking her head, as if her experience of life had been a deep one. "Susie Perkins came to school today with a lovely red carnelian ring. I wanted it dreadfully, and wished I was her with all my might. Well, she drew a picture of Mr. Davis, with a monstrous nose and a hump, and the words, 'Young ladies, my eye is upon you!" coming out of his mouth in a balloon thing. We were laughing over it when all of a sudden his eye *was* on us, and he ordered Susie to bring up her slate. She was *parrylized* with fright, but she went, and oh, what do you think he did! He took her by the ear—the ear! Just fancy how horrid! Then he led her to the recitation platform, and made her stand there half an hour, holding that slate so everyone could see."

"Did the girls laugh at the picture?" asked Jo.

"Laugh? Not one! They sat as still as mice, and Susie cried quarts, I know she did. I didn't envy her then, for I felt that millions of carnelian rings wouldn't have made me happy after that. I never, never should have got over such an agonizing mortification."

"I saw something that I liked this morning, and I meant to tell it at dinner, but I forgot," said Beth, putting Jo's topsy-turvy basket in order as she talked. "When I went to get some oysters for Hannah, Mr. Laurence was in the fish shop. He didn't see me, for I kept behind a barrel, and he was busy with Mr. Cutter the fisherman. A poor woman came in with a pail and a mop, and asked Mr. Cutter if he would let her do some scrubbing for a bit of fish, because she hadn't any dinner for her children, and couldn't get work. Mr. Cutter was in a hurry, and said 'No' rather crossly. She was going away, looking hungry and sorry, when Mr. Laurence hooked up a big fish with the crooked end of his cane and held it out to her. She was so glad and surprised she took it right in her arms, and thanked him over and over. He told her to 'go along and cook it,' and she hurried off, so happy! Wasn't it good of him? Oh, she did look so funny, hugging the big, slippery fish, and wishing Mr. Laurence a soft bed in heaven."

When they had laughed at Beth's story, they asked their mother for one, and, after a moment's thought, she said soberly, "As I sat cutting out blue flannel jackets today at work, I worried about Father, and thought how lonely and helpless we should be if anything happened to him. It was not a wise thing to do, but I kept on worrying till an old man came in with an order for some clothes. He sat down near me, and I began to talk to him, for he looked poor and tired and anxious.

" 'Do you have sons in the army?' I asked.

" 'Yes, ma'am. I had four, but two were killed, one is a prisoner, and I'm going to the other, who is very sick in a Washington hospital,' he answered quietly.

" 'You have done a great deal for your country, sir.'

" 'Not a mite more than I ought, ma'am. I'd go myself, if I was any use. As I ain't, I give my boys, and give 'em free.'

"I'd given one man and thought it too much, while he gave four without grudging them. I had all my girls to comfort me at home, and his last son was waiting, miles away, to say goodbye to him, perhaps! I felt so rich, so happy, thinking of my blessings, that I gave him some money, and thanked him for the lesson he had taught me."

After a moment's silence, Jo said, "Tell another story, Mother—one with a moral to it, like this. I like to think about them afterward, if they are real and not too preachy."

Mrs. March smiled and began at once, for she had told stories to this little audience for many years, and knew how to please them.

"Once upon a time, there were four girls, who had enough to eat and drink and wear, a good many comforts and pleasures, kind friends and parents who loved them dearly, and yet they were not contented." (Here the listeners stole sly looks at one another, and began to sew diligently.) "These girls were anxious to be good and made many excellent resolutions, but they did not keep them very well, and were constantly saying, 'If we only had this,' or, 'If we could only do that,' quite forgetting how much they already had, and how many pleasant things they actually could do. So they asked an old woman what spell they could use to make them happy, and she said, 'When you feel discontented, think over your blessings, and be grateful.' " (Here Jo looked up quickly, as if about to speak, but changed her mind, seeing that the story was not done yet.)

"Being sensible girls, they decided to try her advice, and soon were surprised to see how well off they were. One discovered that money couldn't keep shame and sorrow out of rich people's houses; another that, though she was poor, she was a great deal happier with her youth, health, and cheer, than a certain fretful, feeble old lady; a third that, disagreeable as it was to help get dinner, it was harder still to have to go begging for it; and the fourth, that even carnelian rings were not so valuable as good behavior. So they agreed to stop complaining, to enjoy the blessings already possessed, and try to deserve them; and I believe they were never disappointed or sorry that they took the old woman's advice."

"Now, Marmee, that is cunning of you to turn our own stories against us, and give us a sermon!" cried Meg.

"I like that kind of sermon. It's the sort Father used to tell us," said Beth thoughtfully.

"I don't complain near as much as the others do, and I shall be more careful than ever now," said Amy.

"We needed that lesson, and we won't forget it," added Jo.

5

BEING NEIGHBORLY

"WHAT IN THE WORLD are you going to do now, Jo?" asked Meg one snowy afternoon, as her sister came tramping through the hall in rubber boots, with a broom in one hand and a shovel in the other.

"Going out for exercise," answered Jo with a mischievous twinkle in her eyes.

"I should think two long walks this morning would have been enough! It's cold out, and I advise you to stay warm and dry by the fire, as I do," said Meg with a shiver.

"Never take advice! Can't keep still all day, and not being a pussycat, I don't like to doze by the fire. I like adventures, and I'm going to find some."

Meg went back to toast her feet and read *Ivanhoe*, and Jo began to dig paths with great energy. The snow was light, and with her broom she soon swept a path all round the garden for Beth to walk in when the sun came out and the invalid dolls needed air. The Marches' shabby old brown house stood next to the stately stone mansion of Mr. Laurence in a suburb of the city which was still countrylike, with groves and lawns, large gardens, and quiet streets.

Laurie had not been seen lately, and Jo began to think he had gone away, until one day she spied a brown face at an upper window, looking wistfully down into their garden, where Beth and Amy were snow-balling one another. She said to herself. "His grandpa does not know what's good for him, and keeps him shut up all alone. He needs some-body young and lively. I've a great mind to go over and tell the old gentleman so!"

Jo saw Mr. Laurence drive off, and then sallied out to dig her way down to the hedge, where she paused and took a survey. All quiet—curtains down at the lower windows, servants out of sight, and nothing human visible but Laurie's curly black head leaning on a thin hand at the upper window.

"There he is," thought Jo, "poor boy! All alone and sick this dismal day. It's a shame! I'll toss up a snowball and make him look out, and then say a kind word to him."

Up went a handful of soft snow, and the head turned at once, show-ing a face which lost its listless look in a minute, as the big eyes bright-ened and the mouth began to smile. Jo nodded and laughed, and flourished her broom as she called out, "How do you do! Are you sick?"

Laurie opened the window, and croaked out as hoarsely as a raven, "Better, thank you. I've had a bad cold, and been shut up a week."

"I'm sorry. What do you amuse yourself with?"

"Nothing. It's as dull as tombs up here."

"Have someone come and see you, then."

"There isn't anyone I'd like to see. Boys make such a racket, and my head hurts."

"Isn't there some nice girl who'd read and amuse you? Girls are quiet and like to play nurse."

"Don't know any."

"You know us," began Jo, then laughed.

"So I do! Will you come, please?" cried Laurie.

"I'm not quiet and nice, but I'll come, if Mother will let me. I'll go ask her. Shut that window, like a good boy, and wait till I come."

Jo soon appeared next door, looking rosy and kind and quite at her ease, with a covered dish in one hand and Beth's three kittens in the other.

"Here I am, bag and baggage," she said briskly. "Mother sent her love, and was glad if I could do anything for you. Meg wanted me to bring some of her blancmange, she makes it very nicely. And Beth thought her cats would be comforting. I knew you'd laugh at them, but I couldn't refuse, she was so anxious to do something."

It so happened that Beth's funny kittens were just the thing to make Laurie forget his bashfulness.

"That looks too pretty to eat," he said, smiling with pleasure as Jo uncovered the dish, and showed the blancmange pudding, surrounded by a garland of green leaves, and the scarlet flowers of Amy's pet geranium.

"It's so soft, it will slip down without hurting your sore throat. What a cozy room this is!"

"It might be if it was kept nice, but the maids are lazy."

"I'll right it up in two minutes, for it only needs to have the hearth brushed, so—and the things made straight on the mantel-piece, so—and the books put here, and the bottles there, and your sofa turned from the light, and the pillows plumped up a bit. Now, then, you're fixed."

And so he was. For, as she laughed and talked, Jo had whisked things into place and given a different air to the room. Laurie watched her in respectful silence, and when she beckoned him to his sofa, he sat down with a sigh of satisfaction, saying gratefully, "How kind you are! Yes, that's what it needed. Now please take the big chair and if you don't mind, let's talk."

"Not a bit. I'll talk all day if you'll only set me going. Beth says I never know when to stop."

"Is Beth the rosy one, who stays at home a good deal and sometimes goes out with a little basket?" asked Laurie with interest.

"Yes, that's Beth. She's my girl, and a regular good one she is, too."

"The pretty one is Meg, and the curly-haired one is Amy, I believe?"

"How did you find that out?"

Laurie reddened, but answered frankly, "Why, you see, I often hear you calling to one another, and when I'm alone up here, I can't help looking over at your house, you always seem to be having such good times. I beg your pardon for being so rude, but sometimes you forget to pull the curtains at the window where the flowers are. When the lamps are lighted, it's like looking at a picture to see the fire, and you all around the table with your mother—her face looks so sweet behind the flowers—I can't help watching it. I haven't got any mother, you know." And Laurie poked the fire to hide a little twitching of the lips that he could not control.

The solitary, hungry look in his eyes went straight to Jo's warm heart. Her face was friendly and her sharp voice unusually gentle as she said, "We'll never draw that curtain anymore, and I give you permission to look as much as you like. I just wish, though, instead of peeping, you'd come over and see us. Mother is so splendid, she'd do you heaps of good, and Beth would sing to you if I begged her to, and Amy would dance. Meg and I would make you laugh over our funny stage properties, and we'd have jolly times. Wouldn't your grandpa let you?"

"I think he would, if your mother asked him," began Laurie, brightening more and more. "He's afraid I might be a bother to strangers."

"We are not strangers, we are neighbors, and you needn't think you'd be a bother. We *want* to know you."

After a little pause, the boy asked, "Do you like your school?"

"I don't go to school. I'm a businessman—girl, I mean. I go to wait on my great-aunt, and a dear, cross old soul she is, too," answered Jo. She gave him a lively description of the fidgety old lady, her fat poodle, the parrot that talked Spanish, and the library. Laurie enjoyed that immensely. And when she told about the prim old gentleman who came once to woo Aunt March, and, in the middle of a fine speech, how Poll had tweaked his wig off to his great dismay, the boy lay back and laughed till the tears ran down his cheeks, and a maid popped her head in to see what was the matter.

"Oh! That does me no end of good. Keep going," he said, taking his face out of the sofa cushion, red and shining with merriment.

Much elated with her success, Jo told all about their plays and plans, their hopes and fears for Father, and the most interesting events of the little world in which the sisters lived. Then they got to talking about books, and to Jo's delight, she found that Laurie loved them as well as she did, and had read even more than herself.

"If you like them so much, come down and see ours. Grandpa is out, so you needn't be afraid," said Laurie, getting up.

"I'm not afraid of anything," returned Jo, with a toss of the head.

"I don't believe you are!" exclaimed the boy, looking at her with much admiration, though he privately thought she would have good reason to be a trifle afraid of the old gentleman, if she met him in some of his moods.

Laurie led the way from room to room, letting Jo stop to examine whatever struck her fancy. At last they came to the library, where she clapped her hands and pranced, as she always did when especially delighted. It was lined with books, and there were pictures and statues, and little cabinets full of coins and curiosities, and a great open fireplace with quaint tiles all round it.

"What richness!" sighed Jo, sinking into the depth of a velvet chair and gazing about her with an air of intense satisfaction. "Theodore Laurence, you ought to be the happiest boy in the world," she added impressively.

"A fellow can't live on books," said Laurie, shaking his head as he perched on a table opposite.

They heard someone enter the front door, and Jo exclaimed, "Mercy me! It's your grandpa!"

"Well, what if it is! You are not afraid of anything, you know," returned the boy, looking wicked.

"The doctor to see you, sir," and the maid beckoned as she spoke.

"Would you mind if I left you for a minute? I suppose I must see him," said Laurie.

"Don't mind me. I'm as happy as a cricket here," answered Jo.

Laurie went away, and his guest amused herself in her own way. She was standing before a fine portrait of the old gentleman when the door opened again, and, without turning, she said firmly, "I'm sure now that I shouldn't be afraid of him, for he's got kind eyes, though his mouth is grim, and he looks as if he had a tremendous will of his own. He isn't as handsome as my grandfather, but I like him."

"Thank you, ma'am," said a gruff voice behind her, and there, to her great dismay, stood old Mr. Laurence.

Poor Jo blushed till she couldn't blush any redder, and her heart began to beat uncomfortably fast as she thought what she had said. The old gentleman said abruptly, after the dreadful pause, "So you're not afraid of me, hey?"

"Not much, sir."

"And you don't think me as handsome as your grandfather?"

"Not quite, sir."

"And I've got a tremendous will, have I?"

"I only said I thought so."

"But you like me in spite of it?"

"Yes, I do, sir."

That answer pleased the old gentleman: "You've got your grandfather's spirit, if you haven't his face. He *was* a fine man, my dear. But, what is better, he was a brave and honest one, and I was proud to be his friend."

"Thank you, sir."

"What have you been doing to this boy of mine, hey?" was the next question, sharply put.

"Only trying to be neighborly, sir." And Jo told how her visit came about.

"You think he needs cheering up a bit, do you?"

"Yes, sir. He seems a little lonely, and young folks would do him good perhaps. We are only girls, but we should be glad to help if we could, for we don't forget the splendid Christmas present you sent us," said Jo eagerly.

"Tut, tut, tut. I shall come and see your mother some fine day. Tell her so. There's the tea bell. We have our tea early on the boy's account. Come down and go on being neighborly."

"If you'd like to have me, sir."

"Shouldn't ask you, if I didn't." And Mr. Laurence offered her his arm with old-fashioned courtesy.

"What *would* Meg say to this?" thought Jo, as she was marched away, while her eyes danced with fun as she imagined herself telling the story at home.

Laurie came running downstairs and halted with surprise at the astonishing sight of Jo arm in arm with his grandfather.

"I didn't know you'd come, sir," he began, as Jo gave him a triumphant little glance.

"That's evident, by the racket you made. Come to your tea, sir, and behave like a gentleman."

The old gentleman did not say much as he drank his four cups of tea, but he watched the young people chat away like old friends, and the change in his grandson did not escape him. There was color, light, and life in the boy's face now.

She's right, the lad's lonely. I'll see what these little girls can do for him, thought Mr. Laurence, as he looked and listened.

After tea, Laurie said he had something more to show her, and took her away to the greenhouse, which had been lighted for her benefit. It seemed fairylike to Jo, as she went up and down the walks, enjoying the blooming walls on either side, the soft light, the damp sweet air, and the wonderful vines and trees that hung about her, while her new friend cut the finest flowers till his hands were full. Then he tied them up, saying, with the happy look Jo liked to see, "Please give these to your mother, and tell her I like the medicine she sent me very much."

They found Mr. Laurence standing before the fire in the great drawing room, where Jo's attention was entirely absorbed by a grand piano, which stood open. She asked Laurie if he played.

So Laurie played and Jo listened, with her nose luxuriously buried in heliotrope and tea roses. She praised his music until his grandfather interrupted. "That will do, that will do, young lady. Too many sugarplums are not good for him. His music isn't bad, but I hope he will do as well in more important things. Going? Well, I'm much obliged to you, and I hope you'll come again. My respects to your mother. Good night, Doctor Jo."

He shook hands kindly, but looked displeased. When they got into the hall, Jo asked Laurie if she had said anything wrong, and he explained that his grandfather didn't like to hear him play the piano. Then Jo said good night to Laurie and hurried home.

When Jo had reported her afternoon's adventures, Mrs. March wanted to talk about her father with the old man, Meg longed to walk in the greenhouse, Beth sighed for the grand piano, and Amy was eager to see the fine pictures and statues.

"Mother, why didn't Mr. Laurence like to have Laurie play?" asked Jo.

"I am not sure, but I think it was because his son, Laurie's father, married an Italian lady. The lady was a lovely musician, but he did not like her, and never saw his son after he married her. They both died when Laurie was a little child. I fancy the boy is not very strong, and the old man is afraid of losing him, which makes him so careful. I dare say his grandfather fears that he may want to be a musician like his mother."

"Dear me, how romantic!" exclaimed Meg.

"How silly!" said Jo. "Let him be a musician if he wants to, and not plague his life out sending him to college if he hates to go."

"That's why he has such handsome black eyes and perfect manners, I suppose. Italians are always nice," said Meg, who was a little sentimental.

"What do you know about his eyes and his manners? You hardly spoke to him," scoffed Jo, who was not sentimental.

"I saw him at the party, and what you tell shows that he is a charmer. That was a nice little speech about the medicine Mother sent him."

"He meant the blancmange, I suppose."

"How stupid you are! He meant you, of course."

"Did he?" And Jo opened her eyes wide.

"I never saw such a girl! You don't know a compliment when you get it," said Meg, with the air of a young lady who knew all about the matter.

"I think they are great nonsense, and I'll thank you not to be silly and spoil my fun. Laurie's a nice boy and I like him, and I won't have any sentimental stuff about compliments and such rubbish. He *may* come over and see us, mayn't he, Marmee?"

"Yes, Jo, your young friend is welcome, and I hope Meg will remember that children should be children as long as they can."

"I don't call myself a child anymore, and I'm not even in my teens yet," observed Amy. "What do you say, Beth?"

"I was thinking about our 'Pilgrim's Progress,' " answered Beth, who had not heard a word. "How we have got out of the sad swamp and through the little gate by planning to be good, and up the steep hill by trying hard. Maybe the house over there, full of splendid things, is going to be our Palace Beautiful."

"We have to get by some lions first," said Jo, as if she rather liked that part of the story.

6
BETH FINDS THE PALACE BEAUTIFUL

THE BIG HOUSE did prove a Palace Beautiful, though Beth found it hard to get past the two lions. The biggest one, old Mr. Laurence, said something funny or kind to each one of the girls and talked over old times with their mother, and after that nobody felt much afraid of him except timid Beth. The other lion was the fact that they were poor, and they didn't like to accept favors which they could not return. But Laurie was so grateful for Mrs. March's motherly welcome, their cheerful friendship, and his pleasure in their humble home, that they soon forgot their pride.

The new friendship flourished like grass in spring. Everyone liked Laurie, and he was always running over to the Marches'. Mr. Brooke, Laurie's tutor, finally told Mr. Laurence that Laurie was neglecting his studies.

"Never mind, let him take a holiday, and make it up afterward," said the old gentleman. "Let him do what he likes, as long as he is happy. He can't get into mischief in that little nunnery over there, and Mrs. March is doing more for him than we can."

What good times they had, to be sure! Plays, sleigh rides and skating frolics, pleasant evenings in the old parlor, and now and then little parties in the great stone house. Meg could walk in the greenhouse and pick bouquets, Jo browsed in the library, Amy copied pictures and enjoyed beauty to her heart's content, and Laurie acted like lord of the manor.

But timid Beth could not pluck up courage to go to the "Mansion of Bliss," as Meg called it. She went once with Jo, but the old gentleman stared so hard and said "Hey!" so loud that she declared she would never go there anymore, not even to see the piano. No urging could overcome her fear, until Mr. Laurence heard about the problem and mended matters. During a brief visit to the Marches, he started chatting about great singers he had seen and fine organs he had heard. Beth crept nearer and nearer, then stood listening at the back of his chair, with her great eyes wide open. Taking no more notice of her than if she had been a fly, Mr. Laurence talked on about Laurie's music lessons and presently, as if the idea had just occurred to him, he said to Mrs. March, "The boy neglects his music now, and I'm glad, for he was getting too fond of it. But the piano suffers for want of use. Wouldn't some of your girls like to run over, and practice on it now and then, just to keep it in tune?"

Beth took a step forward, and pressed her hands tightly together to keep from clapping them, for the thought of practicing on that splendid instrument took her breath away. Before Mrs. March could reply, Mr. Laurence went on with an odd little nod and smile, "They needn't see or speak to anyone, but run in at any time; for I'm shut up in my study at the other end of the house, Laurie is out a great deal, and the servants are never near the drawing room after nine o'clock."

He rose, as if going. "Please tell the young ladies what I say, and if they don't care to come, why, never mind."

Beth looked up at him and said, "Oh sir, they do care, very much! I'm Beth. I love it dearly, and I'll come, if you are quite sure nobody will hear me—and be disturbed," she added, fearing to be rude, and trembling at her own boldness as she spoke.

"Not a soul, my dear. The house is empty half the day. So come and drum away as much as you like, and I shall be obliged to you."

Beth blushed like a rose under the friendly look he wore, but she was not frightened now. The old gentleman softly stroked the hair off her forehead and stooped down to kiss her, saying in a tone few people ever heard, "I had a little girl once, with eyes like these. God bless you, my dear! Good day, madam." And away he went, in a great hurry.

Beth rushed up to impart the glorious news to her family of invalids, as her sisters were not at home. Next day, having seen both the old and young gentlemen leave the house, Beth got in at their side door, and made her way as noiselessly as any mouse to the drawing room where her idol stood. Quite by accident, of course, some pretty, easy music lay on the piano, and with trembling fingers and frequent stops to listen and look about, Beth at last touched the great instrument, and straightway forgot her fear, herself, and everything else but the unspeakable delight the music gave her, for it was like the voice of a beloved friend.

She stayed till Hannah came to take her home to dinner; but she had no appetite, and could only sit and smile upon everyone in a general state of bliss.

After that, her little brown hood slipped through the hedge nearly every day. She never knew that Mr. Laurence often opened his study door to hear her old-fashioned songs. She never saw Laurie stand guard in the hall to shoo the servants away. She never suspected that the music books she found in the rack were put there especially for her. Her wish come true was all she had hoped, which isn't always the case.

One day Beth said, "Mother, I'm going to make Mr. Laurence a pair of slippers. He is so kind to me, I must thank him, and I don't know any other way. Can I do it?" Mrs. March took special pleasure in granting Beth's requests because she so seldom asked anything for herself.

After many serious discussions with Meg and Jo, the pattern was chosen, the materials bought, and the slippers begun. A cluster of pansies on a deep purple background was the chosen design, and Beth worked away early and late, with occasional help on the hard parts. Then she wrote a short, simple note, and got Laurie to smuggle them onto the study table one morning before the old gentleman was up.

All that day passed and a part of the next before any acknowledgment arrived, and she was beginning to fear she had offended her crotchety friend. On the afternoon of the second day, she went out to do an errand and give poor Joanna, the invalid doll, her daily exercise. As she came up the street, on her return, she saw four heads popping in and out of the parlor windows with several hands waving, and several joyful voices screamed, "Here's a letter! Come quick, and read it!"

At the door her sisters seized and bore her to the parlor in a triumphal procession, all pointing and all saying at once, "Look there! Look there!" Beth did look, and turned pale with delight and surprise, for there stood a little cabinet piano, with a letter lying on the glossy lid, directed like a sign board to "Miss Elizabeth March."

"For me!" gasped Beth, holding on to Jo and feeling as if she should tumble down, it was such an overwhelming thing altogether.

"Yes, all for you, my precious! Isn't it splendid of him! Don't you think he's the dearest old man in the world! Here's the piano key in the letter. We didn't open it, but we are dying to know what he says," cried Jo, hugging her sister and offering the note.

"You read it! I can't, I feel so faint! Oh, it is too lovely!" And Beth hid her face in Jo's apron, quite upset by her present.

Jo opened the paper and began to laugh, for the first words she saw were

Miss March,
Dear Madam,

I have had many pairs of slippers in my life, but I never had any that suited me so well as yours.

The pansy is my favorite flower, and these will always remind me of the gentle giver. I like to pay my debts, so I know you will allow "the old gentleman" to send you something which once belonged to the little granddaughter he lost. With hearty thanks and best wishes, I remain

Your grateful friend and humble sevant,

James Laurence

"There, Beth, that's an honor to be proud of, I'm sure! Laurie told me how fond Mr. Laurence used to be of the child who died, and how he kept all her little things carefully. Just think, he's given you her piano. That comes of having big blue eyes and loving music," said Jo, trying to soothe Beth, who trembled and looked more excited than she had ever been before.

"See the cunning brackets to hold candles, and the nice green silk, puckered up, with a gold rose in the middle, and the pretty rack and stool, all complete," added Meg, opening the instrument and displaying its beauties.

" 'Your humble servant, James Laurence.' Only think of his writing that to you. I'll tell the girls. They'll think it splendid," said Amy, much impressed by the note.

"Try it, honey. Let's hear the sound of the baby piano," said Hannah, who always took a share in the family joys and sorrows.

So Beth tried it, and everyone pronounced it the most remarkable piano ever heard. It had evidently been newly tuned and put in apple-pie order, but, perfect as it was, the real charm of it lay in the happiest face which leaned over it, as Beth lovingly touched the beautiful black and white keys and pressed the bright pedals.

"You'll have to go and thank him," said Jo as a little joke, for the idea of the shy child's really going never entered her head.

"Yes, I mean to. I guess I'll go now, before I get frightened thinking about it." And, to the utter amazement of the whole family, Beth

So Beth tried it,
and everyone pronounced it the most remarkable piano ever heard.

walked deliberately down the garden, through the hedge, and in at the Laurences' door.

"Well, I wish I may die if it ain't the strangest thing I ever see! The piano has bewitched her! She'd never have gone in her right mind," cried Hannah, staring after her, while the girls were rendered speechless by the miracle.

They would have been still more amazed if they had seen what Beth did afterward. If you will believe me, she went and knocked at the study door before she gave herself time to think, and when a gruff voice called out, "Come in!" she did go in, right up to Mr. Laurence, who looked taken aback, and held out her hand, saying, with only a small quaver in her voice, "I came to thank you, sir, for . . ." But she didn't finish, for he looked so friendly that she forgot her speech and, only remembering that he had lost the little girl he loved, she put both arms round his neck and kissed him.

If the roof of the house had suddenly flown off, the old gentleman wouldn't have been more astonished. But he liked it—oh, dear, yes, he liked it amazingly! He was so touched and pleased by that little kiss that all his crustiness vanished. He set her on his knee, and laid his wrinkled cheek against her rosy one, feeling as if he had his own little granddaughter back again. Beth ceased to fear him from that moment, and sat there talking to him as cozily as if she had known him all her life, for love casts out fear. When she went home, he walked with her to her own gate, shook hands cordially, and touched his hat as he marched back again, looking stately and erect, like a handsome, soldierly old gentleman, as he was.

When the girls saw that performance, Jo began to dance a jig, Amy nearly fell out of the window in her surprise, and Meg exclaimed, with uplifted hands, "Well, I do believe the world is coming to an end!"

7

AMY'S VALLEY
OF HUMILIATION

"THAT BOY IS A PERFECT CYCLOPS, isn't he?" said Amy, one day, as Laurie clattered by on horseback, with a flourish of his whip as he passed.

"How dare you say so, when he's got both his eyes? And handsome ones they are, too," cried Jo, who resented any slighting remarks about her friend.

"I didn't say anything about his eyes, and I don't see why you need to flare up when I admire his riding."

"Oh, my goodness! The little goose means a *centaur,* and she called him a *Cyclops*," exclaimed Jo, with a burst of laughter. (A centaur is a man who is half horse, and a Cyclops is an ugly giant with one eye.)

"You needn't be so rude, it's only a lapse of lingy, as Mr. Davis says," retorted Amy, getting the Latin wrong. "I just wish I had a little of the money Laurie spends on that horse," she added, as if to herself, yet hoping her sisters would hear. "I need it because I'm dreadfully in debt."

"In debt, Amy? What do you mean?" Meg looked sober.

"Why, I owe my friends at least a dozen pickled limes, and I can't pay them back, you know, till I have money, for Marmee forbade my having anything charged at the shop."

"Tell me all about it. Are limes the fad now?" And Meg tried to keep a straight face, Amy looked so grave and important.

"Why, you see, the girls are always buying them, and unless you want to be thought stingy, you must do it, too. It's nothing but limes now, for everyone is sucking them in their desks in schooltime, and trading them off for pencils, bead rings, paper dolls, or something else, at recess. If one girl likes another, she gives her a lime. If she's mad at her, she eats one in front of her and doesn't offer even a suck. They treat by turns, and I've had ever so many but haven't returned them, and I ought, for I'm obligated, you know."

"How much will pay them off, and restore your credit?" asked Meg, taking out her purse.

"A quarter would more than do it, and leave a few cents over for a treat for you. Do you like limes?"

"Not much. You may have my share. Here's the money. Make it last as long as you can, for I don't have much, you know."

"Oh, thank you! It must be so nice to have pocket money! I'll have a grand feast, for I haven't tasted a lime this week. I felt delicate about taking any, as I couldn't return them, and I'm actually suffering for one."

Next day Amy was a bit late to school, but could not resist the temptation of displaying, with pardonable pride, a moist brown-paper parcel, before she consigned it to the inmost recesses of her desk. During the next few minutes the rumor spread that Amy March had twenty-four delicious limes (she ate one on the way) and was going to treat, and the attentions of her friends became overwhelming. Katy Brown invited her to her next party on the spot. Mary Kingsley insisted on lending her her watch till recess. Jenny Snow, a heartless young lady who had twitted Amy upon her limeless state, promptly buried the hatchet and offered to furnish answers to certain math problems. But Amy had not forgotten Miss Snow's cutting remarks about "some persons whose noses were not too flat to smell other people's limes" and "stuck-up people who were not too proud to ask for them." She instantly crushed her hopes with the withering message, "You needn't be so polite all of a sudden, for you won't get any."

A distinguished personage happened to visit the school that morning, and Amy's beautifully drawn maps received praise, which rankled in the soul of Miss Snow and caused Miss March to assume the airs of a studious young peacock. But, alas, alas! Pride goes before a fall, and the revengeful Miss Snow turned the tables with disastrous success. No sooner had the guest left than Jenny, under pretense of asking an important question, whispered to Mr. Davis, the teacher, that Amy March had pickled limes in her desk.

Mr. Davis had declared limes illegal in class and solemnly vowed to publicly swat the hands of the first person who was found breaking the law. He had succeeded in banishing chewing gum after a long and stormy war, had made a bonfire of the confiscated novels and magazines, had stopped the note-passing, had forbidden cartoons, and done all that one man could do to keep half a hundred rebellious girls in order. Boys are hard enough to human patience, goodness knows, but girls are infinitely more so, especially to nervous gentlemen with tyrannical tempers and no talent for teaching.

It was a most unfortunate moment for denouncing Amy, and Jenny knew it. Mr. Davis had evidently taken his coffee too strong that morning, there was an east wind which affected his neuralgia, and his pupils had not impressed his guest so well as he felt he deserved: therefore, to use the language of his schoolgirls, "he was as nervous as a witch and as cross as a bear." The word *limes* was like fire to gunpowder, his yellow face flushed, and he rapped on his desk with an energy which made Jenny rush back to her seat.

"Young ladies, attention, if you please!"

The buzz ceased, and fifty pairs of eyes were obediently fixed upon his awful countenance. "Miss March, come to the desk."

Amy rose to obey, with the limes weighing upon her conscience.

"Bring with you the limes you have in your desk."

"Don't take all," whispered her neighbor, with presence of mind.

Amy hastily shook out half a dozen and laid the rest down before Mr. Davis, feeling that any man possessing a human heart would relent when that delicious fragrance met his nose. Unfortunately, Mr. Davis particularly detested the odor of the popular pickle, and disgust added to his wrath.

"Is that all?"

"Not quite," stammered Amy.

"Bring the rest immediately."

With a despairing glance at her friends, she obeyed.

"You are sure there are no more?"

"I never lie, sir."

"So I see. Now take these disgusting things two by two, and throw them out of the window."

Scarlet with shame and anger, Amy went to and fro six dreadful times, as each doomed pair of pickles—looking oh! so plump and juicy—fell from her reluctant hands. One passionate lime-lover burst into tears.

As Amy returned from her last trip, Mr. Davis gave an ominous "Hem!" and said, in his most impressive manner, "Young ladies, you remember what I said to you a week ago. I am sorry this has happened, but I never allow my rules to be infringed, and I never break my word. Miss March, hold out your hand."

Amy put both hands behind her, turning on him an imploring look which pleaded for her better than words. She was a favorite of his, and it's likely he would have broken his word if one irrepressible young lady had not uttered a faint hiss. That hiss sealed the culprit's fate.

"Your hand, Miss March!" Too proud to cry or beg, Amy set her teeth, threw back her head defiantly, and bore without flinching several tingling swats of his ruler on her palm. They were neither many nor heavy, but that made no difference to her. For the first time in her life she had been struck, and the disgrace, in her eyes, was as deep as if he had knocked her down.

"You will now stand on the platform till recess," said Mr. Davis, resolved to do the thing thoroughly that he had begun.

It would have been bad enough to go to her seat, and see the pitying faces of her friends and the satisfied faces of her few enemies. But to stand before the class with that shame seemed impossible, and for a second she felt as if she could only drop down where she stood, and break her heart with crying. She fixed her eyes on the stove funnel and stood there, so motionless and white that the girls found it hard to study with that pathetic figure before them.

During the fifteen minutes that followed, the proud and sensitive little girl suffered a shame and pain which she never forgot. To others it might seem a trivial affair, but during the twelve years of her life she had been governed by love alone, and a blow of that sort had never touched her before. The sting of her hand was forgotten in the sting of the thought, "I shall have to tell at home, and they will be so disappointed in me!"

The fifteen minutes seemed an hour, but they came to an end at last, and the word "Recess!" had never seemed so welcome to her before.

"You can go, Miss March," said Mr. Davis, looking uncomfortable.

Amy gave him a reproachful glance and went without a word straight into the cloakroom, snatched her things, and left "forever," as she passionately declared to herself. She was in a sad state when she got home, and when the older girls arrived, some time later, an indignation meeting was held at once. Mrs. March did not say much, but looked disturbed. Meg bathed the hurt hand with glycerine and tears, Beth felt that even her beloved kittens would fail to cheer Amy, Jo wrathfully proposed that Mr. Davis be arrested without delay, and Hannah shook her fist at the "villain" and pounded potatoes for dinner as if she had him in the bowl.

Mr. Davis was kindly in the afternoon, also unusually nervous. Just before school closed, Jo appeared, wearing a grim expression as she stalked up to the desk and delivered a letter from her mother, then collected Amy's property and departed, carefully scraping the mud from her boots on the door mat as if she shook the dust of the place off her feet.

"Yes, you can have a vacation from school, but I want you to study a little every day with Beth," said Mrs. March that evening. "I don't approve of corporal punishment, especially for girls. I dislike Mr. Davis's manner of teaching and don't think the girls you associate with are doing you any good, so I shall ask your father's advice before I send you anywhere else."

"That's good! I wish all the girls would leave, and spoil his old school. It's perfectly maddening to think of those lovely limes," sighed Amy.

"I am not sorry you lost them, for you broke the rules and deserved some punishment for disobedience." That disappointed the young lady, who expected nothing but sympathy.

"Do you mean you are glad I was disgraced before the whole school?"

"I would not have chosen that way of mending a fault," replied her mother, "but it may do you much good. You are getting to be rather conceited, my dear. You have a good many little talents, but there is no need of parading them. There is not much danger that real quality will be overlooked long; and even if it is, the joy of having it and using it should be enough. The charm of talent is modesty."

"So it is!" cried Laurie, who was playing chess in a corner with Jo. "I knew a girl once who had a remarkable talent for music and composed sweet things when she was alone. But she didn't know it and wouldn't have believed it if anyone had told her."

"I wish I'd known that nice girl. Maybe she would have helped me, I'm so stupid," said Beth, who stood beside him, listening eagerly.

"You do know her, and she helps you better than anyone else could," answered Laurie, looking at her with such mischievous meaning in his merry black eyes that Beth suddenly turned red and hid her face in the sofa cushion, overcome by such an unexpected compliment.

Jo let Laurie win the game. Beth was too overcome to play the piano, so Laurie did his best, and sang delightfully. When he was gone, Amy said suddenly, as if busy over some new idea, "Laurie isn't conceited, is he?"

"Not in the least. That is why we all like him so much."

"I see. It's nice to have accomplishments and be elegant, but not to show off," said Amy thoughtfully.

"Talents can be seen and felt in a modest person," said Mrs. March, "without making a display of them."

"Any more than it's proper to wear all your bonnets and gowns and ribbons at once, that folks may know you've got them," added Jo, and the lecture ended in a laugh.

8
JO MEETS HER DEMON

"GIRLS, WHERE ARE YOU GOING?" asked Amy, coming into their room one Saturday afternoon, and finding them getting ready to go out with an air of secrecy which excited her curiosity.

"Never mind. Little girls shouldn't ask questions," returned Jo sharply.

Turning to Meg, who never refused her anything very long, Amy said coaxingly, "Do tell me! I should think you might let me go, too, for Beth is fussing over her piano, and I don't have anything to do, and am so lonely."

"I can't, dear, because you aren't invited," began Meg, but Jo broke in impatiently, "Now, Meg, be quiet or you will spoil it all. You can't go, Amy, so don't be a baby and whine about it."

"You are going somewhere with Laurie—I know you are. You were whispering and laughing together on the sofa last night, and you stopped when I came in. Aren't you going with him?"

"Yes, we are. Now do be still, and stop bothering."

Amy held her tongue, but used her eyes, and saw Meg slip a fan into her pocket.

"I know! I know! You're going to the theater to see *Seven Castles!*" she cried, adding resolutely, "and I shall go, for Mother said I might see it.

I've got my money, and it was mean not to tell me in time."

"Just listen to me and be a good child," said Meg soothingly. "Mother doesn't wish you to go this week, because you are not well enough yet. Next week you can go with Beth and Hannah, and have a nice time."

"Please let me go now. I've been sick with this cold so long, and shut up, I'm dying for some fun. Do, Meg! I'll be ever so good," pleaded Amy, looking as pathetic as she could.

"Suppose we take her. I don't believe Mother would mind, if we bundle her up well," began Meg.

"If she goes I shan't; and if I don't, Laurie won't like it. It will be rude, after he invited only us, to go and drag in Amy. I should think she'd hate to poke herself where she isn't wanted," said Jo crossly, for she disliked the trouble of overseeing a fidgety child when she wanted to enjoy herself.

Her tone and manner angered Amy, who began to put her boots on, saying, in her most aggravating way, "I shall go. Meg says I may, and if I pay for myself, Laurie hasn't anything to do with it."

"You can't sit with us, for our seats are reserved!" snapped Jo, crosser than ever, having just pricked her finger in her hurry.

Sitting on the floor with one boot on, Amy began to cry. Laurie called from below, and the two girls hurried down, leaving their sister wailing; for now and then she forgot her grown-up ways and acted like a spoiled child. She got up and called over the banisters, "You'll be sorry for this, Jo March, see if you ain't."

"Fiddlesticks!" returned Jo, slamming the door.

The Seven Castles of the Diamond Lake was as brilliant and wonderful as a heart could wish. But between the acts Jo amused herself with wondering what her sister would do to make her "sorry for it." She and Amy had had many lively skirmishes in the course of their lives, for both had quick tempers. Amy teased Jo, and Jo irritated Amy. Although the oldest, Jo had the least self-control and had hard times trying to curb her anger. Her sisters used to say that they liked to get Jo into a fury because she was such an angel afterward.

When they got home, they found Amy reading in the parlor. She never lifted her eyes from her book. On going up to put away her best hat, Jo's first look was toward the bureau, for in their last quarrel Amy had soothed her feelings by turning Jo's top drawer upside down on the floor. Everything was in its place, however, and after a hasty glance into her various closets, bags, and boxes, Jo decided that Amy had forgiven and forgotten her wrongs.

There Jo was mistaken, for next day she made a discovery. Late in the afternoon Jo burst in on Meg, Beth, and Amy, demanding breathlessly, "Has anyone taken my book?"

Meg and Beth said, "No," at once, and looked surprised. Amy poked the fire and said nothing. Jo was down upon her in a minute.

"Amy, you have it!"

"No, I haven't."

"You know where it is, then!"

"No, I don't."

"That's a fib!" cried Jo, taking her by the shoulders, and looking fierce enough to frighten a much braver child than Amy.

"It isn't. I haven't got it, don't know where it is now, and don't care."

"You know something about it, and you'd better tell at once, or I'll make you." And Jo gave her a slight shake.

"You'll never see your silly old book again," cried Amy.

"Why not?"

"I burned it up."

"What? My little book I worked over and meant to finish before Father got home? Have you really burned it?" said Jo, turning pale.

"Yes, I did! I told you I'd make you pay for being so cross yesterday, and I have, so . . ."

Amy got no further, for Jo shook her till her teeth chattered in her head, crying in a passion of grief and anger. "You wicked, wicked girl! I never can write it again, and I'll never forgive you as long as I live."

Meg flew to rescue Amy, but Jo was beside herself. With a parting whack on her sister's ear, she rushed out of the room.

Mrs. March came home and soon brought Amy to a sense of the wrong she had done her sister. Jo's book was the pride of her heart. It was only half a dozen little fairy tales, but Jo had put her whole heart into her work, hoping to make something good enough to print. Amy's bonfire had consumed the loving work of several years.

When the tea bell rang, Jo appeared, looking so grim and unapproachable that it took all Amy's courage to say meekly, "Please forgive me, Jo. I'm very, very sorry."

"I never shall forgive you" was Jo's stern answer, and from that moment she ignored Amy entirely.

All had learned by experience that when Jo was in that mood words were wasted, and the wisest course was to wait. It was not a happy evening. As Jo received her good-night kiss, Mrs. March whispered gently, "My dear, don't let the sun go down upon your anger. Forgive each other, help each other, and begin again tomorrow."

Jo blinked hard, shook her head, and said gruffly because Amy was listening, "It was an abominable thing, and she doesn't deserve to be forgiven." With that she marched off to bed.

The next day Jo still looked like a thundercloud, and nothing went well. It was bitter cold in the morning, she dropped her turnover in the gutter, Aunt March had an attack of fidgets, Beth looked grieved when she got home, and Amy kept making remarks about people who were always talking about being good and yet wouldn't try.

"Everybody is so hateful, I'll ask Laurie to go skating. He is always kind and jolly, and will put me to rights, I know," said Jo to herself, and off she went.

Amy heard the clash of skates, and looked out with an impatient exclamation. "There! She promised I should go next time, for this is the last ice we shall have. But it's no use to ask such a crosspatch to take me."

"Don't say that. You were very naughty, and it is hard to forgive the loss of her precious book. But I think she might do it now," said Meg. "Go after them. Don't say anything till Jo has got good-natured with Laurie, then I'm sure she'll be friends again."

"I'll try," said Amy, and after a flurry to get ready, she ran after the friends, who were just disappearing over the hill.

It was not far to the river. Jo saw Amy coming, and turned her back. Laurie did not see, for he was carefully skating along the shore, checking the ice.

"I'll go on to the first bend, and see if it's all right before we begin to race." He shot away, looking like a young Russian in his fur-trimmed coat and cap.

Jo heard Amy panting, stamping her feet, and blowing her fingers as she tried to put her skates on. But Jo never turned and went slowly zigzagging down the river, taking a bitter, unhappy sort of satisfaction in her sister's troubles. She had cherished her anger till it took possession of her, as evil thoughts and feelings always do unless cast out at once.

As Laurie turned the bend, he shouted back, "Keep near the shore! It isn't safe in the middle."

Amy was just struggling to her feet and did not catch a word. Jo glanced over her shoulder, and the little demon she was harboring said in her ear, "No matter whether she heard or not, let her take care of herself."

Laurie had vanished round the bend, Jo was just at the turn, and Amy headed out toward the smoother ice in the middle of the river. Jo had a strange feeling in her heart, then decided to go on. But something turned her around just in time to see Amy throw up her hands and go down, with the sudden crash of thin ice, the splash of water, and a cry that made Jo's heart stand still with fear. She tried to call Laurie, but her voice was gone. She tried to rush forward, but her feet seemed to have no strength in them. For a second, she could only stand motionless, staring with a terror-stricken face at the little blue hood above the black water.

Something rushed swiftly by her, and Laurie's voice cried out, "Bring a fence rail. Quick, quick!"

How she did it, she never knew. For the next few minutes she worked as if possessed, blindly obeying Laurie, who was in control. Lying flat, he held Amy up till Jo dragged a rail from the fence, and together they got the child out, more frightened than hurt.

"Now then, we must walk her home as fast as we can. Pile our things on her, while I get off these confounded skates," cried Laurie, wrapping his coat around Amy, and tugging away at the straps, which never seemed so intricate before.

Shivering, dripping, and crying, they got Amy home, and after an exciting time of it, she fell asleep, rolled in blankets before a hot fire. During the bustle Jo had scarcely spoken but flown about, looking pale and wild, with her things half off, her dress torn, and her hands cut and bruised by ice and fence rails and skate buckles. When Amy was comfortably asleep, the house quiet, and Mrs. March sitting by the bed, she called Jo to her and began to bandage the hurt hands.

"Are you sure she is safe?" whispered Jo, looking remorsefully at the golden head which might have been lost forever under the treacherous ice.

"Quite safe, dear. She is not hurt, and won't even take cold, I think, you were so sensible in covering and getting her home quickly."

"Laurie did it all. Mother, if she should die, it would be my fault." And Jo dropped down beside the bed in a passion of penitent tears, telling all that had happened. "It's my dreadful temper! I try to cure it. I think I have, and then it breaks out worse than ever. Oh, Mother, what shall I do? What shall I do?"

"Watch and pray, dear. Never get tired of trying, and never think it is impossible to conquer your fault," said Mrs. March, drawing Jo's head to her shoulder and kissing the wet cheek so tenderly that Jo cried harder than ever.

"You don't know, you can't guess how bad it is! It seems as if I could do anything when I'm in a passion. I get so savage, I could hurt anyone and enjoy it. I'm afraid I shall do something dreadful some day, and spoil my life. Oh, Mother, help me, do help me!"

"Jo, dear, we all have our temptations, some far greater than yours, and it often takes us all our lives to conquer them. You think your temper is the worst in the world, but mine used to be just like it."

"Yours, Mother? Why, you are never angry!"

"I've been trying to cure it for forty years, and have only succeeded in controlling it. I am angry nearly every day of my life, Jo, but I have learned not to show it. I still hope to learn not to feel it, though it may take me another forty years to do so."

"Mother, are you angry when you press your lips tight together and go out of the room sometimes, when Aunt March scolds or people pester you?" Jo felt nearer and dearer to her mother than ever before.

"Yes, I've learned to hold back the words that rise to my lips, and when I feel that they might break out against my will, I just go away a minute, and give myself a little shake," answered Mrs. March with a sigh and a smile, as she smoothed and fastened up Jo's disheveled hair.

"How did you learn to keep still? That is what troubles me. The sharp words fly out before I know it, and the more I say the worse I get, till it's a pleasure to hurt people's feelings and say dreadful things. Tell me how you do it, Marmee dear."

"My good mother used to help me, but I lost her when I was a little older than you are. I had a hard time, Jo. Then your father came, and I was so happy that I found it easy to be good-natured. But by-and-by, when I had four little daughters round me and we were poor, then the old trouble began again, for I am not patient by nature."

"Poor Mother! What helped you then?"

"Your father, Jo. He never doubts or complains, but always hopes, and works and waits so cheerfully that one is ashamed to do otherwise before him. He showed me that I must try to practice all the virtues I would like my little girls to possess, for I was their example. It was easier to try for your sakes than for my own."

"Oh, Mother, if I'm ever half as good as you, I shall be satisfied," cried Jo, much touched.

"I hope you will be a great deal better, dear. But you must keep watch over your besetting sin, or it may sadden, if not spoil your life. You have had a warning. Try to master this quick temper, before it brings you greater sorrow and regret than it did today."

"I will try, Mother, I truly will. But you must remind me. I used to see Father sometimes put his finger on his lips, and look at you, and you always pressed your lips tight or went away. Was he reminding you then?" asked Jo softly.

"Yes. I asked him to do it, and he saved me from many a sharp word by that little gesture and kind look."

Jo saw that her mother's eyes filled and her lips trembled, and she whispered anxiously, "Was it wrong to ask about that? It feels so good to say anything at all to you, and feel so safe and happy here."

"My Jo, you may say anything to your mother, for it is my greatest happiness to feel that my girls confide in me and know how much I love them. I got weepy speaking of Father because of how much I miss him."

"Yet you told him to go, Mother, and didn't cry when he went, and never complain now, or seem as if you need any help," said Jo, wondering.

"I gave my best to the country I love, and kept my tears till he was gone. We both have merely done our duty! If I don't seem to need help, it is because I have a better friend, even than Father, to comfort and sustain me. Jo, the troubles and temptations of your life are beginning and may be many, but you can overcome and outlive them all if you learn to feel the strength and tenderness of your heavenly Father. The more you love and trust Him, the nearer you will feel to Him, and the less you will depend on human power and wisdom. His love and care never tire or change, can never be taken from you, but may become the source of lifelong peace, happiness, and strength. Go to God with all your little cares and hopes and sins and sorrows as freely and openly as you come to your mother."

Jo's only answer was to hold her mother close. Then the sincerest prayer she had ever prayed left her heart without words. In that sad yet happy hour, she had learned not only the bitterness of remorse and despair, but the sweetness of trust and obedience. She had drawn nearer to the Friend who offers love stronger than that of any father, tenderer than that of any mother.

Amy stirred and sighed in her sleep, and Jo looked up with an expression on her face which it had never worn before.

"I let the sun go down on my anger. I wouldn't forgive her, and today, if it hadn't been for Laurie, it might have been too late! How could I be so wicked?" said Jo, half aloud, as she leaned over her sister, softly stroking the wet hair scattered on the pillow.

As if she heard, Amy opened her eyes, and held out her arms, with a smile that went straight to Jo's heart. Neither said a word, but they hugged one another close, in spite of the blankets, and everything was forgiven and forgotten.

9

MEG GOES TO VANITY FAIR

"I DO THINK it was the most fortunate thing in the world that those children should have the measles just now," said Meg one April day as she was packing for a vacation, surrounded by her sisters.

"And so nice of Annie Moffat not to forget her promise. Two weeks of fun will be splendid," replied Jo, looking like a windmill as she folded skirts with her long arms.

"And such lovely weather, I'm so glad of that," added Beth, tidily sorting ribbons, lent for the great occasion.

"I wish I was going to have a fine time and wear all these nice things," said Amy. "What did Mother give you out of the treasure box?" Mrs. March kept a few relics of past splendor in her cedar chest, as gifts for her girls when the proper time came.

"A pair of silk stockings, that pretty carved fan, and a lovely blue sash. I wanted Marmee's old violet silk dress, but there isn't time to make it over, so I must be content with my old white muslin."

"The sash will set it off beautifully. I wish I hadn't smashed my coral bracelet, for you might have worn it," said Jo, who loved to give and lend, but whose possessions were usually too dilapidated to be of much use.

"You always look like an angel in white," said Amy, brooding over

Meg's little pile of finery. The girls truly admired her things, but they had to admit that her bonnet and umbrella and most of what she had were the wrong colors or the wrong styles or worn out.

"I wonder if I shall ever be happy enough to have lace on my clothes!" Meg complained.

"You said the other day that you'd be perfectly happy if you could only go to Annie Moffat's," observed Beth in her quiet way.

"So I did! Well, it does seem as if the more one gets the more one wants, doesn't it?" said Meg, cheering up, as she glanced from the half-filled trunk to the many-times-pressed-and-mended white muslin.

The next day was fine, and Meg departed in style for two weeks of novelty and pleasure. Mrs. March had reluctantly consented to the visit, fearing that Margaret would come back more discontented than she went. But she had begged so hard, and a little pleasure seemed so delightful after a winter of irksome work that the mother yielded, and the daughter went to take her first taste of fashionable life.

The Moffats were kindly people, and soon put their guest at ease. It certainly was agreeable to eat sumptuously, drive in a fine carriage, wear her best frock every day, and do nothing but enjoy herself. It suited her exactly, and soon she began to imitate the manners and conversation of those about her, to put on little airs and graces, use French phrases, curl her hair, and talk about fashions as well as she could. The more she saw of Annie Moffat's pretty things, the more she envied her and sighed to be rich. Home now looked bare and dismal as she thought of it, work seemed harder than ever, and she felt that she was a destitute and much-injured girl, in spite of the new gloves and silk stockings.

The three young girls (for Sallie Gardiner was also a guest of the Moffats) were busily employed in "having a good time." They shopped, walked, rode, and paid visits all day, and went to theaters and operas or entertained friends in the evening. The older sisters were fine young ladies, and one was engaged, which seemed extremely romantic. Meg enjoyed Mr. Moffat, a fat, jolly old gentleman who knew her father, and Mrs. Moffat, a fat, jolly old lady. Everyone called Meg "Daisy" and flattered her.

When the evening for the party came, Meg brought out her muslin, looking older, limper, and shabbier than ever beside Sallie's crisp new one. Meg saw the girls glance at it and then at one another, and her cheeks began to burn. No one said a word about it, but in their kindness Meg saw only pity for her poverty; and her heart felt heavy while the others laughed, chattered, and flew about like gauzy butterflies. The hard, bitter feeling was getting pretty bad, when the maid brought in a box of flowers. Annie pulled the cover off, and all were exclaiming at the lovely roses, heath, and fern within.

" 'They are for Miss March,' the man said. And here's a note," put in the maid, holding it out to Meg.

"What fun! Who are they from? We didn't know you had a lover," cried the girls, fluttering about Meg in a high state of curiosity and surprise.

"The note is from Mother, and the flowers from Laurie," said Meg.

"Oh, indeed!" said Annie with a funny look.

Feeling almost happy again, Meg saved a few ferns and roses for herself, and quickly made up the rest in dainty corsages for her friends.

She enjoyed herself that evening, for she danced to her heart's content; everyone was kind, and she had three compliments. Annie made her sing, and someone said she had a remarkably fine voice. Major Lincoln asked who "the fresh little girl with the beautiful eyes" was, and Mr. Moffat insisted on dancing with her because she "didn't dawdle, but had some spring in her." So altogether she had a nice time, till she overheard a bit of conversation.

She was sitting just inside the greenhouse, waiting for her dance partner to bring her an ice cream, when she heard a voice ask on the other side of the flowery wall, "How old is he?"

"Sixteen or seventeen, I should say," replied another voice.

"It would be a grand thing for one of those girls, wouldn't it? Sallie says the old man dotes on them."

"Mrs. M. has made her plans, I dare say, and will play her cards well, early as it is," said Mrs. Moffat.

"She told that fib about her mamma sending the note, and blushed when the flowers came. Poor thing! She'd be so nice if she was only got up in style. Do you think she'd be offended if we offered to lend her a dress for Thursday?" asked another voice.

"She's proud, but I don't believe she'd mind, for that dowdy muslin is all she has. She may tear it tonight, and that will be a good excuse for offering her a decent one."

Here Meg's partner appeared, to find her looking agitated. She could not understand the gossip of her friends. She tried to forget it, but could not, and kept repeating to herself, "Mrs. M. has made her plans," "that fib about her mamma," and "dowdy muslin," until she was ready to cry and rush home. As that was impossible, she did her best to seem happy, and being rather excited, she succeeded very well.

She was glad when it was all over and she was quiet in her bed, where she could think and cry. A new world had opened to Meg, and much disturbed the peace of the old one in which till now she had lived as happily as a child. Her faith in her mother was a little shaken by the worldly plans attributed to her by Mrs. Moffat, who judged others by herself; and the sensible resolution to be contented with the simple wardrobe which suited a poor man's daughter was weakened by the pity of girls who thought a shabby dress one of the greatest calamities under heaven.

Poor Meg had a restless night, and got up half ashamed of herself for not speaking out frankly and setting everything right. Something in the manner of her friends struck Meg at once: they treated her with more respect, she thought, took a tender interest in what she said, and looked at her with eyes that plainly betrayed curiosity. Finally Miss Belle looked up from her writing, and said, with a sentimental air,

"Daisy, dear, I've sent an invitation to your friend, Mr. Laurence, for Thursday. We should like to meet him."

Meg blushed, but a mischievous urge to tease the girls made her reply demurely, "You are very kind, but I'm afraid he won't come."

"Why not?" asked Miss Belle.

"He's too old."

"What do you mean? What is his age?" cried Miss Clara.

"Nearly seventy, I believe," answered Meg.

"You sly creature! Of course we meant the young man," exclaimed Miss Belle, laughing.

"There isn't any, Laurie is only a little boy." Meg laughed at the strange look the sisters exchanged as she described her supposed lover.

"About your age," Nan said.

"Nearer my sister Jo's. I am seventeen in August," returned Meg, tossing her head.

"It's nice of him to send you flowers, isn't it?" said Annie.

"Yes, he often does, to all of us, for their house is full, and we are so fond of them. My mother and old Mr. Laurence are friends, you know."

"I'm going out to get some little matters for my girls; can I do anything for you, young ladies?" asked Mrs. Moffat, lumbering in like an elephant in silk and lace.

"No, thank you, ma'am," replied Sallie. "I've got my new pink silk for Thursday and don't need a thing."

"Nor I . . ." began Meg, but stopped because it occurred to her that she did need several things and could not have them.

"What shall you wear?" asked Sallie.

"My old white one again, if I can mend it fit to be seen. It got sadly torn last night," said Meg, feeling uncomfortable.

"Why don't you send home for another?" said Sallie.

"I don't have any other."

Belle broke in, saying kindly, "What is the use of having a lot of dresses? There's no need of sending home, Daisy, even if you had a dozen, for I've got a sweet blue silk laid away, which I've outgrown, and you shall wear it to please me, won't you, dear?"

"You are very kind, but I don't mind my old dress if you don't. It does well enough for a young girl like me," said Meg.

"Do let me enjoy myself by dressing you up in style. You'd be a regular little beauty with a touch here and there. I shan't let anyone see you till you are done, and then we'll burst upon them like Cinderella and her godmother going to the ball," said Belle in her persuasive tone.

Meg couldn't refuse the offer so kindly made, for a desire to see if she would be "a little beauty" caused her to forget all her uncomfortable feelings toward the Moffats.

On Thursday evening, Belle shut herself up with her maid, and between them they turned Meg into a fine lady. They crimped and curled her hair, touched her lips with coralline salve to make them redder, and would have added a touch of rouge, if Meg had not rebelled. They laced her into a sky-blue dress, which was so tight she could hardly breathe and so low in the neck that modest Meg blushed at herself in the mirror. A set of silver filigree was added, bracelets, necklace, brooch, and even earrings. A cluster of tea-rose buds at the bosom and a pair of high-heeled blue silk boots satisfied the last wish of her heart. A lace handkerchief, a feathery fan, and a bouquet in a silver holder finished her off, and Miss Belle surveyed her with the satisfaction of a little girl with a newly dressed doll.

"Come and show yourself," said Miss Belle, leading the way to the room where the others were waiting. Meg went rustling after, with her long skirts trailing, her earrings tinkling, her curls waving, and her heart beating. The mirror had plainly told her that she was "a little beauty." Her friends were all excited.

"I'm afraid to go down, I feel so strange and stiff and half-dressed," said Meg to Sallie.

"You're quite French, I assure you. Let your flowers hang, don't be so careful of them, and be sure you don't trip," returned Sallie, trying not to care that Meg was prettier than herself.

Margaret got safely downstairs and sailed into the drawing rooms where the Moffats and a few early guests were assembled. She soon discovered that there is a charm about fine clothes which attracts certain people and secures their respect. Several young ladies who had taken no notice of her before, were very affectionate; several young gentlemen who had only stared at her at the other party, now asked to be introduced and said all manner of agreeable things to her; and several old ladies, who sat on sofas and criticized the rest of the party, inquired who she was with an air of interest. She heard Mrs. Moffat reply to one of them, "Daisy March—father a colonel in the army—one of our first families, but reverses of fortune, you know; intimate friends of the Laurences. A sweet girl, I assure you. My Ned is wild about her."

"Dear me!" said the old lady, putting on her glasses for another look at Meg, who was shocked at Mrs. Moffat's fibs.

She imagined herself acting the new part of fine lady, though the tight dress gave her a side-ache. She was flirting with her fan and laughing at the feeble jokes of a young gentleman who tried to be witty, when she suddenly stopped laughing, for she saw Laurie. He was staring at her with undisguised surprise. Although he bowed and smiled, something in his honest eyes made her blush and wish she had her old dress on. She saw Belle nudge Annie, and both glance from her to Laurie, who, she was happy to see, looked unusually boyish and shy.

Meg rustled across the room to shake hands with her friend. "I'm glad you came. I was afraid you wouldn't," she said, with her most grown-up air.

"Jo wanted me to come and tell her how you looked, so I did," answered Laurie, without turning his eyes upon her, though he half smiled.

"What shall you tell her?" asked Meg, full of curiosity.

"I shall say I didn't know you, for you look so grown-up and unlike yourself, I'm quite afraid of you," he said, fumbling at his glove button.

"How absurd of you! The girls dressed me up for fun, and I rather like it. Wouldn't Jo stare if she saw me?" said Meg, bent on making him say whether he thought her improved or not.

"Yes, I think she would," returned Laurie gravely.

"Don't you like me so?" asked Meg.

"No, I don't" was the blunt reply.

"Why not?" in an anxious tone.

He glanced at her frizzled head, bare shoulders, and fantastically trimmed dress with an expression that abashed her even more than his answer, which had not a particle of his usual politeness about it.

"I don't like fuss and feathers."

That was altogether too much from a lad younger than herself, and Meg walked away, saying petulantly, "You are the rudest boy I ever saw."

Feeling ruffled, she went and stood at a quiet window to cool her cheeks. As she stood there, Major Lincoln passed by, and a minute later she heard him saying to his mother, "They are making a fool of that little girl; I wanted you to see her, but they have spoiled her entirely; she's nothing but a doll tonight."

She leaned her forehead on the cool pane, and stood half hidden by the curtains, never minding that her favorite waltz had begun, till someone touched her. Turning, she saw Laurie, looking penitent. He said, with his best bow and his hand out, "Please forgive my rudeness, and come and dance with me."

"I'm afraid it will be too disagreeable to you," said Meg, trying to look offended and failing entirely.

"Not a bit of it. Come, I'll be good. I don't like your gown, but I do think you are . . . just splendid." And he waved his hands, as if words failed to express his admiration.

Meg smiled and relented, and whispered as they stood waiting to catch the time, "Take care my skirt doesn't trip you up; it's the plague of my life and I was a goose to wear it."

"Pin it round your neck, and then it will be useful," said Laurie, looking down at the little blue boots, which he evidently approved of. Away they went fleetly and gracefully, having practiced at home. They twirled merrily round and round, feeling more friendly than ever after their small tiff.

"Laurie, I want you to do me a favor, will you?" said Meg, as he stood fanning her when her breath gave out, which it did very soon though she would not admit why. "Please don't tell them at home about my dress tonight. They won't understand the joke, and it will worry Mother. I shall tell them myself all about it, and 'fess' to Mother how silly I've been. But I'd rather do it myself; so you'll not tell, will you?"

"I give you my word I won't, only what shall I say when they ask me?"

"Just say I looked pretty well and was having a good time."

"I'll say the first with all my heart, but how about the other? You don't look as if you were having a good time. Are you?"

And Laurie looked at her with an expression which made her answer in a whisper, "No, not just now. Don't think I'm horrid. I only wanted a little fun, and I'm getting tired of it."

"Here comes Ned Moffat. What does he want?" said Laurie, knitting his black brows.

"He put his name down for three dances, and I suppose he's coming for them. What a bore!" said Meg, assuming a languid air which amused Laurie immensely.

He did not speak to her again till suppertime, when he saw her drinking champagne with Ned and his friend Fisher. He felt a brotherly sort of right to watch over the Marches.

"You'll have a splitting headache tomorrow if you drink much of that. I wouldn't, Meg. Your mother doesn't like it, you know," he whispered, leaning over her chair, as Ned turned to refill her glass and Fisher stooped to pick up her fan.

They twirled merrily round and round,
feeling more friendly than ever after their small tiff.

"I'm not Meg tonight. I'm 'a doll' who does all sorts of crazy things. Tomorrow I shall put away my fuss and feathers and be desperately good again," she answered with a tense little laugh.

"I wish tomorrow was here, then," muttered Laurie.

Meg was sick all the next day, and on Saturday went home, quite used up with her two weeks of fun, and feeling that she had "sat in the lap of luxury" long enough.

"It does seem pleasant to be quiet, and not have company manners on all the time. Home is a nice place, though it isn't splendid," Meg said, looking about her with a restful expression, as she sat with her mother and Jo on Sunday evening.

"I'm glad to hear you say so, dear, for I was afraid home would seem dull and poor to you now." Her mother had given her many anxious looks that day, for motherly eyes are quick to see any change in children's faces.

When the younger girls were gone to bed, Meg sat thoughtfully staring at the fire, saying little. As the clock struck 9:00, Meg suddenly left her chair and, taking Beth's stool, leaned her elbows on her mother's knee, saying bravely, "Marmee, I want to 'fess.' "

"I thought so. What is it, dear?"

"Shall I go away?" asked Jo discreetly.

"Of course not. Don't I always tell you everything? I was ashamed to speak of it before the children, but I want you to know all the dreadful things I did at the Moffats'. I told you they dressed me up, but I didn't tell you that they powdered and squeezed and frizzled, and made me look like a fashion plate. Laurie thought I wasn't proper, though he didn't say so, and one man called me 'a doll.' I knew it was silly, but they flattered me and said I was a beauty, and quantities of nonsense."

"Is that all?" asked Jo, as Mrs. March looked silently at the downcast face of her pretty daughter, and could not find it in her heart to blame her little follies.

"No, I drank champagne and tried to flirt, and was altogether abominable," said Meg self-reproachfully.

"There is something more, I think."

"Yes. It's silly, but I want to tell it." Then she told the gossip about the Marches she had overheard at the Moffats', and as she spoke, Jo saw her mother press her lips tightly.

"Well, if that isn't the greatest rubbish I ever heard," cried Jo indignantly. "Why didn't you pop out and tell them so on the spot?"

"I couldn't, it was so embarrassing for me. I couldn't help hearing at first, and then I was so angry and ashamed."

"Just wait till I see Annie Moffat, and I'll show you how to settle such ridiculous stuff. The idea of having 'plans,' and being kind to Laurie because he's rich and may marry us by-and-by!" And Jo laughed.

"Forget it as soon as you can," said Mrs. March gravely. "I was unwise to let you go among people of whom I know so little—kind, I dare say, but worldly, ill-bred, and full of these vulgar ideas about young people."

"Don't be sorry, I won't let it hurt me. I'll forget all the bad and remember only the good, for I did enjoy a great deal, and thank you very much for letting me go. It was nice to be praised and admired, and I can't help saying I like it," said Meg, looking half ashamed of the confession.

"That is perfectly natural, and quite harmless, if the liking does not lead one to do foolish things. But learn to know and value the praise which is worth having. The admiration of excellent people comes by being modest as well as pretty, Meg."

Jo stood with her hands behind her, looking both interested and a little perplexed, for it was a new thing to see Meg blushing and talking about admiration, lovers, and things of that sort. Jo felt as if during that fortnight her sister had grown up amazingly, and was drifting away from her into a world where she could not follow.

"Mother, do you have 'plans,' as Mrs. Moffat said?" asked Meg bashfully.

"Yes, my dear, I have a great many, but mine differ somewhat from Mrs. Moffat's. I will tell you some of them. I want my daughters to be beautiful, accomplished, and good; to be admired, loved, and respected; to have a happy youth, to be well and wisely married, and to lead useful, pleasant lives, with as little care and sorrow as God sees fit to send. My dear girls, I am ambitious for you, but not to have you marry rich men merely because they are rich, or have splendid houses which are not homes because love is missing. Money is a needful and precious thing—and, when well used, a noble thing—but I never want you to think it is the first or only prize to strive for. I'd rather see you poor men's wives, if you were happy, beloved, and contented, than queens on thrones, without self-respect and peace."

"Poor girls don't stand any chance, Belle says, unless they put themselves forward," sighed Meg.

"Then we'll be old maids," said Jo stoutly.

"Right, Jo. It's better to be happy old maids than unhappy wives, or unmaidenly girls, running about to find husbands," said Mrs. March decidedly. "Leave these things to time. Make this home happy, so that you may be ready for homes of your own, if they are offered you. One thing remember: Mother is always ready to be your confidante, Father to be your friend, and both of us trust and hope that, whether married or single, you will be the pride and comfort of our lives."

"We will, Marmee, we will!" cried both, with all their hearts, as she said good night.

10

THE PICKWICK CLUB
AND THE POST OFFICE

As SPRING CAME ON, the lengthening days gave long afternoons for work and play of all sorts. The garden had to be put in order, and each sister had a quarter of the little plot with which to do what she liked. Hannah used to say, "I'd know which girl each of them gardens belonged to, ef I seed 'em in China"; and so she might, for the girls' tastes differed as much as their characters.

Meg's had roses and heliotrope, myrtle, and a little orange tree in it. Jo's was never alike two seasons, for she was always trying experiments. This year it was to be a plantation of sunflowers; the seeds were to feed Aunt Cockletop and her family of chicks. Beth had old-fashioned fragrant flowers in her garden—sweet peas and mignonette, larkspur, pinks, pansies, and southernwood, with chickweed for the bird and catnip for the kitties. Amy had a bower in hers—small and buggy, but pretty to look at—with honeysuckles and morning-glories hanging their colored horns and bells in graceful wreaths all over it, tall white lilies, delicate ferns, and as many brilliant, picturesque plants as would consent to blossom there.

Gardening, walks, rows on the river, and flower hunts filled the sunny days; and for rainy ones, they had indoor activities—some old, some new—all more or less original. One of these was the "P.C."

Because secret societies were the fashion, they felt they should have one; and as all of the girls admired Dickens, they copied his novel *The Pickwick Papers* and called themselves the Pickwick Club. With a few interruptions, they had kept this up for a year, and met every Saturday evening in the big garret. Three chairs were arranged in a row before a table on which was a lamp, four white badges with a big 'P.C.' in different colors on each, and a weekly club newspaper called *The Pickwick Portfolio.*

At seven o'clock, the four members ascended to the clubroom, put on their badges, and took their seats with great solemnity. Meg, as the eldest, played the part of Samuel Pickwick; Jo, being literary, played Augustus Snodgrass; Beth, being round and rosy, played Tracy Tupman; and Amy, who was always trying to do what she couldn't, played Nathaniel Winkle. Pickwick, the president, read their newspaper aloud. They all contributed something, and Jo was the editor. The paper was filled with original tales, poetry, local news, funny advertisements, and hints, in which they good-naturedly reminded each other of their faults and shortcomings.

On one occasion, "Mr. Pickwick" put on a pair of glasses without any lenses, rapped upon the table, hemmed, and, having stared hard at "Mr. Snodgrass," who was tilting back in his chair, began to read the May 20 edition of *The Pickwick Portfolio.* First came the "Poet's Corner," with an ode by Jo (A. Snodgrass) that began:

> Again we meet to celebrate
> > With badge and solemn rite,
> Our fifty-second anniversary
> > In Pickwick Hall tonight.

Next came a romantic tale set in Venice, by Meg (S. Pickwick), titled "The Masked Marriage." It told how the beautiful Lady Viola escaped a forced marriage to Count Antonio, whom she hated, and wed instead her artist lover Ferdinand Devereux. This was followed by "The History of a Squash" by Beth (T. Tupman), which told how a little girl bought a squash for her mother, lugged it home, cut it up, boiled it in a big pot, and mashed some of it with salt and butter for dinner—"to the rest she added a pint of milk, two eggs, four spoons of sugar, nutmeg, and some crackers; put it in a deep dish, and baked it until it was brown and nice; and next day it was eaten by a family named March."

"The Public Bereavement" announced that the beloved Mrs. Snowball Pat Paw was missing for weeks and presumed dead. This announcement was followed by "A Lament for S. B. Pat Paw," which began:

> We mourn the loss of our little pet,
>   And sigh o'er her hapless fate,
> For never more by the fire she'll sit,
>   Nor play by the old green gate.

This was followed by advertisements and a behavior report: "Meg—Good, Jo—Bad, Beth—Very Good, Amy—Middling." As the president finished reading this paper, a round of applause followed, and then "Mr. Snodgrass" rose to make a proposition.

"Mr. President and gentlemen," he began, assuming a parliamentary attitude and tone, "I wish to propose the admission of a new member—one who highly deserves the honor, would be deeply grateful for it, and would add immensely to the spirit of the club, the literary value of the paper, and be no end jolly and nice. I propose Mr. Theodore Laurence as an honorary member of the P.C."

"We'll put it to vote," said the president. "All in favor of this motion please say, 'Aye.' "

A loud response from "Snodgrass," followed, to everybody's surprise, by a timid one from Beth.

"Contrary-minded say, 'No.' "

Meg and Amy were contrary-minded, and "Mr. Winkle" rose to say with great elegance, "We don't wish any boys, they only joke and bounce about. This is a ladies' club, and we wish it to be private and proper."

"I'm afraid he'll laugh at our paper, and make fun of us afterward," observed "Pickwick," pulling the little curl on her forehead, as she always did when doubtful.

Up rose "Snodgrass," much in earnest. "Sir, I give you my word as a gentleman, Laurie won't do anything of the sort. He likes to write, and he'll give a tone to our contributions and keep us from being sentimental, don't you see? We can do so little for him, and he does so much for us, I think the least we can do is to offer him a place here, and make him welcome if he comes."

This brought "Tupman" to his feet, looking as if he had made up his mind. "Yes, we ought to do it, even if we *are* afraid. I say he *may* come, and his grandpa, too, if he likes."

This outburst from Beth electrified the club, and Jo left her seat to shake hands approvingly. "Now then, vote again. Everybody remember it's our Laurie, and say, 'Aye!' " cried "Snodgrass."

"Aye! aye! aye!" replied three voices at once.

"Good! Bless you! Now, allow me to present the new member. . . ." And, to the dismay of the rest of the club, Jo threw open the door of the closet and displayed Laurie, flushed and twinkling with suppressed laughter.

"You rogue! You traitor! Jo, how could you?" cried the three girls, as "Snodgrass" led her friend triumphantly forth, and producing both a chair and a badge, installed him in a jiffy.

The new member said in the most engaging manner, "Mr. President and ladies—I beg pardon, gentlemen—allow me to introduce myself as Sam Weller, the humble servant of the club."

"Good! Good!" cried Jo, pounding with a pan.

"My faithful friend and noble patron," continued Laurie with a wave of the hand, "who has so flatteringly presented me, is not to be blamed for the trick. I planned it, and she only gave in after lots of teasing."

"Come now, don't lay it all on yourself; you know I suggested the closet," broke in "Snodgrass," who was enjoying the joke amazingly.

"Never you mind what she says. I'm the wretch that did it, sir," said the new member. "But on my honor, I never will do so again, and henceforth *devote* myself to the interest of this immortal club."

"Hear! Hear!" cried Jo, clashing the lid of the pan like a cymbal.

Laurie continued, "I merely wish to say that as a slight token of my gratitude for the honor done me, and as a means of promoting friendly relations between adjoining nations, I have set up a post office in the hedge in the lower corner of the garden, a fine, spacious building with padlocks on the doors and every convenience for the mails—also the females, if I may be allowed the expression. It's the old bird house, but I've stopped up the door and made the roof open like a lid, so it will hold all sorts of things, and save our valuable time. Allow me to present the club key, and with many thanks for your favor, take my seat."

Great applause as "Mr. Weller" deposited a little key on the table and sat down. Jo's pan clashed and waved wildly, and it was some time before order could be restored. It was an unusually lively meeting, and did not adjourn till a late hour, when it broke up with three shrill cheers for the new member. No one ever regretted the admittance of "Sam Weller," for a more devoted, well-behaved, and jovial member no club could have. He certainly did add "spirit" to the meetings and a "tone" to the paper, for his speeches convulsed his hearers and his writings were excellent. Jo regarded them as worthy of Milton or Shakespeare.

The P.O. flourished wonderfully, for nearly as many strange things passed through it as through the real post office. Tragedies and neckties, poetry and pickles, garden seeds and long letters, music and gingerbread, galoshes, invitations, scoldings, and puppies. The old gentleman liked the fun, and amused himself by sending odd bundles, mysterious messages, and funny telegrams; and his gardener, who was smitten with Hannah's charms, actually sent a love letter in Jo's care. How they laughed when that secret came out, never dreaming how many love letters that little post office would hold in the years to come!

11
EXPERIMENTS

"The first of June! The Kings are off to the seashore tomorrow, and I'm free. Three months' vacation—how I shall enjoy it!" exclaimed Meg, coming home one warm day. Jo was lying upon the sofa in an unusual state of exhaustion while Beth took off her dusty boots, and Amy made lemonade for the refreshment of the whole group.

"Aunt March left today, for which, oh, be joyful!" said Jo. "I was mortally afraid she'd ask me to go with her. If she had, I should have felt as if I ought to do it, but Plumfield is about as lively as a churchyard, you know. We had a flurry getting the old lady off, and I had a fright every time she spoke to me, for I was in such a hurry to be through that I was uncommonly helpful and sweet, and feared she'd find it impossible to part from me. I quaked till she was in the carriage, and then had a final fright, for as it drove off, she popped out her head, saying, 'Josyphine, won't you? . . .' I didn't hear any more, for I turned and fled. I did actually run, and whisked round the corner where I felt safe."

"Poor old Jo! She came in looking as if bears were after her," said Beth, as she cuddled her sister's feet with a motherly air.

"Aunt March is a regular samphire, isn't she?" observed Amy, tasting her lemonade critically.

"She means *vampire*, but it doesn't matter; it's too warm to be particular," murmured Jo.

"What shall you do all your vacation?" asked Amy, changing the subject.

"I shall lie abed late, and do nothing," replied Meg, from the depths of the rocking chair. "I got up early all winter and had to spend my days working for other people, so now I'm going to rest and relax to my heart's content."

"No," said Jo, "that dozy way wouldn't suit me. I've laid in a heap of books, and I'm going to improve my shining hours reading on my perch in the old apple tree, when I'm not having fun with Laurie."

"Don't let us do any lessons, Beth, for a while, but play all the time and rest," proposed Amy.

"All right, if Mother doesn't mind. I want to learn some new songs, and my children need fixing up for the summer. They are really suffering for clothes."

"May we, Mother?" asked Meg, turning to Mrs. March, who sat sewing in what they called "Marmee's corner."

"You may try your experiment for a week and see how you like it. I think by Saturday night you will find that all play and no work is as bad as all work and no play."

"Oh, dear, no! It will be delicious, I'm sure," said Meg complacently.

"I now propose a toast. Fun forever and no grubbing!" cried Jo, rising, glass in hand, as the lemonade went round.

They all drank it merrily, and began the experiment by lounging for the rest of the day. Next morning, Meg did not appear till ten o'clock. She found that her lonely breakfast did not taste nice and the room seemed untidy, for Jo had not filled the vases, Beth had not dusted, and Amy's books lay scattered about. Nothing was neat and pleasant but "Marmee's corner," which looked as usual. There Meg sat, to "rest and read," which meant yawn and imagine what pretty summer dresses she would buy.

Jo spent the morning on the river with Laurie and the afternoon reading up in the apple tree. Beth began by rummaging everything out of the big closet where her family resided, but getting tired before half done, she left the closet topsy-turvy and went to her music, rejoicing that she had no dishes to wash. Amy arranged her garden bower, put on her best white frock, smoothed her curls, and sat down to draw under the honeysuckles, hoping someone would see and inquire who the young artist was. As no one appeared but an inquisitive daddy long-legs, who examined her work with interest, she went for a walk, got caught in a shower, and came home dripping.

At teatime they compared notes, and all agreed that it had been a delightful, though unusually long day. Meg, who went shopping in the afternoon and got some "sweet blue muslin" cloth, had discovered, after she cut it into sections, that it wouldn't wash, which made her slightly cross. Jo had sunburned her nose boating, and got a raging headache by reading too long. Beth was bothered by the confusion of her closet and the difficulty of learning three or four songs at once; and Amy deeply regretted what the rain did to her frock, for Katy Brown's party was to be the next day and now she had "nothing to wear." But these were mere trifles, and they assured their mother that the experiment was working fine. She smiled, said nothing.

The days kept getting longer and longer, an unsettled feeling possessed everyone, and Satan found plenty of mischief for the idle hands to do. Meg found time hang so heavily that she fell to snipping and spoiling her clothes in her attempts to improve their style. Jo read till her eyes gave out and she was sick of books, even good-natured Laurie had a quarrel with her, and she desperately wished she had gone with Aunt March. Beth got on pretty well, for she was constantly forgetting that it was to be *all play and no work*, and fell back into her old ways now and then, but something in the air affected her. On one occasion she actually shook poor dear Joanna and told her she was "a fright." Amy fared worst of all, for when her sisters left her to amuse and care for herself, she soon found that accomplished and important little self a great burden. One couldn't draw all the time. "If one could have a fine house, full of nice girls, or go traveling, the summer would be delightful, but to stay at home with three selfish sisters and a grown-up boy was enough to try the patience of a Boaz," she complained, after several days devoted to pleasure, fretting, and boredom.

No one would admit that they were tired of the experiment, but by Friday night each acknowledged to herself that she was glad the week was nearly done. Hoping to impress the lesson more deeply, Mrs. March, who had a good deal of humor, resolved to finish off the trial in an appropriate manner, so she gave Hannah a holiday and let the girls enjoy the full effect of the play system.

When they got up on Saturday morning, there was no fire in the kitchen, no breakfast in the dining room, and no mother anywhere to be seen. "Mercy on us! What has happened?" cried Jo, staring about her in dismay.

Meg ran upstairs and soon came back again, looking relieved but rather bewildered, and a little ashamed. "Mother isn't sick, only very tired. She says she is going to stay quietly in her room all day and let us do the best we can. She doesn't act a bit like herself, but she says it has been a hard week for her, so we mustn't grumble but take care of ourselves."

"That's easy enough, and I like the idea. I'm aching for something to do—that is, some new amusement, you know," added Jo quickly.

In fact it was an immense relief to them all to have a little work, and they took hold with a will, but were soon to realize the truth of Hannah's saying, "Housekeeping ain't no joke." There was plenty of food in the larder, and while Beth and Amy set the table, Meg and Jo got breakfast, wondering as they did so why servants ever talked about hard work.

"I shall take some up to Mother, though she said we were not to think of her, for she'd take care of herself," said Meg, who presided and felt matronly behind the teapot.

So a tray was filled before anyone ate, and taken up with the cook's compliments. The boiled tea was bitter, the omelet scorched, and the biscuits speckled with baking soda, but Mrs. March received it all with thanks and laughed heartily over it after Jo was gone.

"Poor little souls, they will have a hard time, I'm afraid, but they won't suffer, and it will do them good," she said, getting out the better food she had provided for herself and disposing of the bad breakfast, so that their feelings might not be hurt—a motherly little deception.

Many were the complaints below, and great Meg's chagrin over her failures. "Never mind, I'll get dinner and be servant; you be hostess and give orders," said Jo, who knew still less than Meg about cooking.

This obliging offer was gladly accepted, and Meg retired to the parlor, which she hastily put in order by whisking the litter under the sofa and shutting the window blinds to save the trouble of dusting. Jo, with perfect faith in her own powers and a friendly desire to make up with Laurie, immediately put a note in the post office, inviting him to dinner at noon.

"You'd better see what you have before you think of having company," said Meg.

"Oh, there's corned beef and plenty of potatoes, and I shall get some asparagus and a lobster. We'll have lettuce and make a salad. I don't know how, but the book tells. I'll have blancmange and strawberries for dessert, and coffee, too, if you want to be elegant."

"Don't try too many messes, Jo, for you can't make anything but gingerbread and molasses candy fit to eat. I wash my hands of the dinner party, and since you have asked Laurie on your own responsibility, you may just take care of him."

"I don't want you to do anything but be polite to him and help with the pudding. You'll give me your advice if I get in a muddle, won't you?" asked Jo, rather hurt.

"Yes, but I don't know much, except about bread and a few trifles. You had better ask Mother before you order anything," returned Meg prudently.

"Of course I shall. I'm not a fool." And Jo went off in a huff at the doubts expressed about her powers.

"Get what you like, and don't disturb me. I'm going out to dinner and can't worry about things at home," said Mrs. March, when Jo spoke to her. "I never enjoyed housekeeping, and I'm going to take a vacation today, and read, write, go visiting, and amuse myself." The unusual spectacle of her busy mother rocking comfortably and reading early in the morning made Jo feel as if some natural phenomenon had occurred, for an eclipse, an earthquake, or a volcanic eruption would hardly have seemed stranger.

"Everything is out of sorts, somehow," she said to herself, going downstairs. "There's Beth crying, that's a sure sign that something is wrong with this family. If Amy is bothering Beth, I'll shake her."

Feeling out of sorts herself, Jo hurried into the parlor to find Beth sobbing over Pip, the canary, who lay dead in the cage with his little claws pathetically extended, as if begging for the food he lacked when he died.

"It's all my fault—I forgot him—there isn't a seed or a drop left. Oh, Pip! Oh, Pip! How could I be so cruel to you?" cried Beth, taking the poor thing in her hands and trying to restore him.

Jo peeped into his half-open eye, felt his little heart, and finding him stiff and cold, shook her head, and offered her domino box for a coffin.

"Put him in the oven, and maybe he will get warm and revive," said Amy hopefully.

"He's been starved, and he shan't be baked now that he's dead. He shall be buried in the garden, and I'll never have another bird, never, my Pip! For I am too bad to own one," murmured Beth, sitting on the floor with her pet folded in her hands.

"The funeral shall be this afternoon, and we will all go. Now, don't cry, Bethy; it's a pity, but nothing goes right this week, and Pip has had the worst of the experiment. Lay him in my box, and after the dinner party we'll have a nice little funeral," said Jo.

Leaving the others to console Beth, she departed to the kitchen, which was in a most discouraging state of confusion. Putting on a big apron, she went to work and got the dishes piled up ready for washing, when she discovered that the fire was out, so there was no hot water.

"Here's a sweet prospect!" muttered Jo, slamming the stove door open, and poking vigorously among the cinders.

Having rekindled the fire, she thought she would go to market while the water heated. The walk revived her spirits, and flattering herself that she had made good bargains, she trudged home again, after buying a young lobster, some old asparagus, and two boxes of strawberries. By the time she got the kitchen clean, the stove was red-hot. Hannah had left a pan of bread to rise; Meg had worked it up early, set it on the hearth for a second rising, and forgotten it. Meg was entertaining Sallie Gardiner in the parlor, when the door flew open and a floury, flushed, and disheveled figure appeared, demanding tartly:

"I say, isn't bread 'riz' enough when it runs over the pans?"

Sallie began to laugh, but Meg nodded and lifted her eyebrows as high as they would go, which caused the apparition to vanish and put the bread into the oven without further delay. Mrs. March went out, after peeping here and there to see how matters went, also saying a word of comfort to Beth, who sat by the dear departed who lay in state in the domino box. A strange sense of helplessness fell upon the girls as the gray bonnet vanished round the corner, and despair seized them when a few minutes later Miss Crocker appeared, and said she'd come to dinner. Now, this lady was a thin, yellow spinster, with a sharp nose and inquisitive eyes, who saw everything and gossiped about all she saw. They disliked her, but had been taught to be kind to her, simply because she was old and poor and had few friends. So Meg gave her the easy chair and tried to entertain her, while she asked questions, criticized everything, and told stories of the people she knew.

The dinner Jo served up became a standing joke. She did her best, and discovered that something more than energy and good will is necessary to make a cook. She boiled the asparagus for an hour and was grieved to find the heads cooked off and the stalks harder than ever. The bread burned black, for the salad dressing so aggravated her that she let everything else go till she had convinced herself that she could not make it fit to eat. The lobster was a scarlet mystery to her, but she hammered and poked till it was unshelled and its meager proportions concealed in a grove of lettuce leaves. The potatoes had to be hurried, not to keep the asparagus waiting, and were not done. The blancmange was lumpy, and the strawberries not as ripe as they looked.

"Well, they can eat beef and bread and butter, if they are hungry, only it's mortifying to have to spend your whole morning for nothing," thought Jo, as she rang the dinner bell half an hour later than usual. Hot and tired, she surveyed the feast spread for Laurie, accustomed to all sorts of elegance, and Miss Crocker, whose curious eyes would mark all failures and whose tattling tongue would report them far and wide.

Poor Jo would gladly have gone under the table, as one thing after another was tasted and left, while Amy giggled, Meg looked distressed, Miss Crocker pursed her lips, and Laurie talked and laughed with all his might to give a cheerful tone to the festive scene. Jo's one strong point was the fruit, for she had sugared it well and had a pitcher of rich cream to eat with it. Her hot cheeks cooled a trifle, and she drew a long breath as the pretty glass plates went round, and everyone looked graciously at the little rosy islands floating in a sea of cream. Miss Crocker tasted first, made a wry face, and drank some water hastily. Jo refused, thinking there might not be enough, and glanced at Laurie; he was eating away manfully, though there was a slight pucker about his mouth and he kept his eye fixed on his plate. Amy, who was fond of delicate fare, took a heaping spoonful, choked, hid her face in her napkin, and left the table in a rush.

"Oh, what is it?" exclaimed Jo, trembling.

"Salt instead of sugar, and the cream is sour," replied Meg with a tragic gesture.

Jo uttered a groan and fell back in her chair, remembering that she had given a last hasty powdering to the berries out of one of the two boxes on the kitchen table, and had neglected to put the milk in the refrigerator. She turned scarlet and was on the verge of crying, when she met Laurie s eyes, which *would* look merry in spite of his heroic efforts. The comical side of the affair suddenly struck her, and she laughed till the tears ran down her cheeks. So did everyone else, even "Croaker," as the girls called the old lady, and the unfortunate dinner ended gaily, with bread and butter, olives and fun.

"I haven't strength of mind enough to clear up now, so we will sober ourselves with a funeral," said Jo, as they rose. Miss Crocker made ready to go, being eager to tell the new story at another friend's dinner table.

They did sober themselves for Beth's sake. Laurie dug a grave under the ferns in the grove, and little Pip was laid in with many tears by his tenderhearted mistress, then covered with moss. A wreath of violets and chickweed was hung on the stone which bore his epitaph, composed by Jo while she struggled with the dinner:

> Here lies Pip Marsh,
> Who died the seventh of June;
> Loved and lamented sore,
> And not forgotten soon.

At the conclusion of the ceremonies, Beth retired to her room, overcome with emotion and lobster, but there was no place to rest, for the beds were not made, and she found her grief much relieved by fluffing up pillows and putting things in order. Meg helped Jo clear away the remains of the feast, which took half the afternoon and left them so tired that they agreed to be contented with tea and toast for supper. Laurie took Amy to drive, which was a deed of charity, for the sour cream seemed to have had a bad effect upon her temper. Mrs. March came home to find the three older girls hard at work in the middle of the afternoon.

Before the housewives could rest, several people called, and there was a scramble to get ready to see them; then tea must be got and errands done. As twilight fell, dewy and still, one by one they gathered on the porch where the June roses were budding beautifully, and each groaned or sighed as she sat down, as if tired or troubled.

"What a dreadful day this has been!" began Jo, usually the first to speak.

"It has seemed shorter than usual, but so uncomfortable," said Meg.

"Not a bit like home," added Amy.

"It can't seem so without Marmee and little Pip," sighed Beth, glancing with full eyes at the empty cage above her head.

"Here's Mother, dear, and you shall have another bird tomorrow, if you want it."

As she spoke, Mrs. March came and took her place among them, looking as if her holiday had not been much pleasanter than theirs. Beth nestled up to her and the rest turned toward her with brightening faces, as flowers turn toward the sun. "Are you satisfied with your experiment, girls, or do you want another week of it?"

"I don't!" cried Jo decidedly.

"Nor I," echoed the others.

"You think, then, that it is better to have a few duties and live a little for others, do you?"

"Lounging and larking doesn't pay," observed Jo, shaking her head. "I'm tired of it and mean to go to work at something right off."

"Suppose you learn plain cooking. That's a useful accomplishment, which no woman should be without," said Mrs. March, laughing inaudibly at the recollection of Jo's dinner party, for she had met Miss Crocker and heard her account of it.

"Mother, did you go away and let everything be, just to see how we'd get on?" cried Meg, who had had suspicions all day.

"Yes, I wanted you to see how the comfort of all depends on each doing her share faithfully. While Hannah and I did your work, you got on pretty well, though I don't think you were very happy or amiable. So I thought, as a little lesson, I would show you what happens when everyone thinks only of herself. Don't you feel that it is more pleasant to help one another, to have daily duties which make leisure sweet when it comes, and to bear and forbear, that home may be comfortable and lovely to us all?"

"We do, Mother, we do!" cried the girls.

"Then let me advise you to take up your little burdens again, for they are good for us, and lighten as we learn to carry them. Work is wholesome, and there is plenty for everyone. It keeps us from boredom and mischief, is good for health and spirits, and gives us a sense of power and independence better than money or fashion."

"We'll work like bees, and love it, too. See if we don't!" said Jo. "I'll learn plain cooking for my holiday task, and the next dinner party I have shall be a success."

"I'll make the set of shirts for Father, instead of letting you do it, Marmee. I can and I will, though I'm not fond of sewing. That will be better than fussing over my own things, which are plenty nice enough as they are," said Meg.

"I'll do my lessons every day, and not spend so much time with my music and dolls. I am a stupid thing, and ought to be studying, not playing," was Beth's resolution, while Amy followed their example by heroically declaring, "I shall learn to make buttonholes, and attend to my parts of speech."

"Very good! Then I am quite satisfied with the experiment—only don't go to the other extreme and work like slaves. Have regular hours for work and play, make each day both useful and pleasant, and prove that you understand the worth of time by using it well. Then youth will be delightful, old age will bring few regrets, and life will become a beautiful success, in spite of poverty."

"We'll remember, Mother!" And they did.

12
CAMP LAURENCE

BETH WAS POSTMISTRESS, for, being most at home, she could attend to it regularly, and liked the daily task of unlocking the little box and distributing the mail. One July day she came in with her hands full, and went about the house leaving letters and parcels like the penny post.

"Here's your posy, Mother! Laurie never forgets that," she said.

"Miss Meg March, one letter and a glove," continued Beth, delivering the articles to her sister, who sat near her mother, stitching wristbands.

"Why, I left a pair over there, and here is only one," said Meg, looking at the gray cotton glove. "Did you drop the other in the garden?"

"No, I'm sure I didn't, for there was only one in the post office."

"I hate to have odd gloves! Never mind, the other may be found. My letter is only a translation of the German song I wanted. I think Mr. Brooke did it, for this isn't Laurie's writing."

Mrs. March glanced at Meg, who was looking very pretty in her gingham dress, with the little curls blowing about her forehead. Mrs. March smiled to herself.

"Two letters for Doctor Jo, a book, and a funny old hat—which was on top, covering the whole post office," said Beth, laughing as she went into the study where Jo sat writing.

"What a sly fellow Laurie is! I said I wished bigger hats were the fashion, because I burn my face every hot day. He said, 'Why mind the fashion! Wear a big hat!' I said I would if I had one, and he has sent me this. I'll wear it for fun, and show him I don't care about fashion."
And hanging the antique sunhat on a bust of Plato, Jo read her letters.

One from her mother made her cheeks glow and her eyes fill, for it said to her:

My dear:
I write a little word to tell you with how much satisfaction I watch your efforts to control your temper. You say nothing about your trials, failures, or successes, and think, perhaps, that no one sees them but the Friend whose help you daily ask. I, too, have seen them all. Go on, dear, patiently and bravely, and always believe that no one sympathizes more tenderly with you than your loving
Mother

Laying her head on her arms, Jo wet her book with a few happy tears, for she had thought that no one saw and appreciated her efforts to be good, and this assurance was doubly precious because unexpected and from the person whose commendation she most valued. She pinned the note inside her frock, as a shield and a reminder, and proceeded to open her other letter. In a big, dashing hand, Laurie wrote:

Dear Jo,

What ho!
Some English girls and boys are coming to see me tomorrow and I want to have a jolly time. If it doesn't rain, I'm going to pitch my tent in Longmeadow, and row up the whole crew to lunch and croquet—have a fire, make messes, gypsy fashion,

and all sorts of fun. The Vaughns are nice people, and like such things. Brooke will go, and I want you all to come!

In a tearing hurry,

Yours ever, Laurie

Jo flew in to tell the news to Meg.

"Do you know anything about them, Jo?" asked Meg.

"Only that there are four of them. Kate is older than you, Fred and Frank (twins) about my age, and a little girl (Grace), who is nine or ten. Laurie knew them abroad, and liked the boys. I fancied, from the way he primmed up his mouth in speaking of her, that he didn't admire Kate much."

"I'm so glad my French print is clean, it's just the thing and so becoming!" observed Meg complacently. "Have you anything decent, Jo?"

"Scarlet and gray boating suit, good enough for me. I shall row and tramp about. You'll come, Beth?"

"If you won't let any of the boys talk to me. I like to please Laurie, and I'm not afraid of Mr. Brooke, he is so kind; but I don't want to play, or sing, or say anything."

"That's my good girl. You do try to fight off your shyness, and I love you for it. Fighting faults isn't easy, as I know. Now let's fly round, and do double duty today, so that we can play tomorrow with free minds," said Jo.

When the sun peeped into the girls' room early next morning to promise them a fine day, he saw a comical sight. Each had made preparation for the festivity. Meg had an extra row of little curlpapers across her forehead, Jo had copiously anointed her sunburnt face with cold cream, Beth had taken Joanna to bed with her to atone for the approaching separation, and Amy had put a clothespin on her nose to uplift it. It was one of the kind artists use to hold the paper on their drawing boards, therefore quite appropriate. This funny spectacle appeared to amuse the sun, for he burst out with such radiance that Jo woke up and roused all her sisters by a hearty laugh at Amy's nose ornament.

Sunshine and laughter were good omens for a pleasure party, and soon a lively bustle began in both houses. Beth, who was ready first, kept reporting what went on next door.

"There goes the man with the tent! I see Mrs. Barker doing up the lunch in a hamper and a great basket. Now Mr. Laurence is looking up at the sky; I wish he would go, too. There's Laurie, looking like a sailor! Oh, mercy me! Here's a carriage full of people—a tall lady, a little girl, and two dreadful boys. One is lame; poor thing, he's got a crutch. Laurie didn't tell us that. Why, there is Ned Moffat!"

"So it is. How odd that he should come. I thought he was at the mountains. There is Sallie. I'm glad she got back in time," cried Meg in a flutter. Then she added, "Oh, Jo, you are not going to wear that? It's too absurd!" as Jo tied down with a red ribbon the broad-brimmed, old-fashioned hat Laurie had sent for a joke.

"It's capital—so shady, light, and big. It will make fun, and I don't mind if I'm comfortable." With that Jo marched straight away and the rest followed—a bright little band of sisters, all looking their best in summer clothes, with happy faces under their jaunty hatbrims.

Laurie ran to present them to his friends. Meg was grateful to see that Miss Kate, though twenty, was dressed with simplicity, and she was much flattered by Mr. Ned's assurances that he came especially to see her. Jo understood why Laurie "primmed up his mouth" when speaking of Kate, for that young lady had a stand-off-don't-touch-me air. Beth took an observation of the new boys and decided that the lame one was not "dreadful," but gentle and feeble, and she would be kind to him on that account. Amy found Grace a well-mannered, merry little person, and after staring silently at one another for a few minutes, they suddenly became good friends.

The two boats pushed off together, leaving Mr. Laurence waving his hat on the shore. Laurie and Jo rowed one boat, Mr. Brooke and Ned the other, while Fred Vaughn, the riotous twin, did his best to upset both by paddling about in a one-man rowboat like a disturbed water bug. Jo's funny hat broke the ice in the beginning by producing a laugh. It flapped to and fro as she rowed, and would make an excellent umbrella for the whole party, if a shower came up, she said. Kate looked amazed at Jo's proceedings, especially as she exclaimed, "Christopher Columbus!" when she lost her oar. But after putting up her eyeglass to examine the peculiar girl several times, Miss Kate decided that she was "odd, but rather clever," and smiled.

Meg, in the other boat, was delightfully situated, face to face with the rowers. Mr. Brooke was a grave, silent young man, with handsome brown eyes and a pleasant voice. Meg considered him a walking encyclopedia of useful knowledge. He never talked to her much, but he looked at her a good deal. Ned, being in college, of course put on all the airs which freshmen think it their duty to assume, and was altogether an excellent person to take on a picnic. Sallie Gardiner was absorbed in keeping her white pique dress clean and chattering with Fred.

"Welcome to Camp Laurence!" said the young host, as they landed with exclamations of delight at a pleasant green field, with three widespreading oaks in the middle and a smooth strip of turf for croquet.

"Brooke is commander in chief, I am commissary general, the other fellows are staff officers, and you, ladies, are company. Now, let's have a game of croquet before it gets hot, and then we'll see about dinner."

Frank, Beth, Amy, and Grace sat down to watch. Mr. Brooke chose Meg, Kate, and Fred; Laurie took Sallie, Jo, and Ned. The English played well, but the Americans played better, as if the spirit of '76 inspired them. Jo and Fred had several skirmishes. Jo was through the last wicket and had missed the stroke. Fred's turn came before hers; he gave a stroke, his ball hit the wicket, and stopped an inch on the wrong side. No one was near, and running up to examine, he gave it a sly nudge with his toe, which put it just an inch on the right side.

"I'm through! Now, Miss Jo, I'll settle you, and get in first," cried the young gentleman, swinging his mallet for another blow.

"You pushed it! I saw you! It's my turn now," said Jo sharply.

"Upon my word, I didn't move it. It rolled a bit, perhaps, but that is allowed. Stand off, please, and let me have a go at the stake."

"We don't cheat in America, but you can, if you choose," said Jo angrily.

"Yankees are the most tricky, everybody knows. There you go!" returned Fred, croqueting her ball far away.

Jo opened her lips to say something rude, but checked herself in time, while Fred hit the stake with much exultation. She went off to get her ball, and was a long time finding it among the bushes, but she came back, looking cool and quiet, and waited her turn patiently. It took several strokes to regain the place she had lost, and when she got there, the other side had nearly won, for Kate's ball was next to last and lay near the stake.

"By George, it's all up! Goodbye, Kate. Miss Jo owes me one, so you are finished," cried Fred excitedly, as they all drew near to see the finish. He thought that Jo was going to knock Kate's ball far away.

"Yankees have a trick of being generous to their enemies," said Jo, "especially when they beat them," she added, as, leaving Kate's ball untouched, she won the game by a clever stroke.

Laurie threw up his hat, then remembered that it wouldn't do to exult over the defeat of his guests, and stopped in the middle of a cheer to whisper to his friend, "Good for you, Jo! He did cheat, I saw him."

Meg drew her aside, under pretense of pinning up a loose braid, and said approvingly, "It was dreadfully provoking, but you kept your temper, and I'm so glad, Jo."

"Don't praise me, Meg, for I could box his ears this minute. I should certainly have boiled over if I hadn't stayed away till I got my rage under enough to hold my tongue," returned Jo, biting her lips as she glowered at Fred from under her big hat.

"Time for lunch," said Mr. Brooke, looking at his watch. "Commissary general, will you make the fire and get water, while Miss March, Miss Sallie, and I spread the table? Who can make good coffee?"

Jo, feeling that her late lessons in cookery were to do her honor, went to preside over the coffeepot, while the children collected dry sticks, and the boys made a fire and got water from a spring near by.

A merry lunch it was, for everything seemed fresh and funny, and frequent peals of laughter startled a venerable horse who fed near by. There was a pleasing tilt in the table, which produced many mishaps to cups and plates. Acorns dropped into the milk, little black ants partook of the refreshments without being invited, and fuzzy caterpillars swung down from the tree to see what was going on.

"There's salt here, if you prefer it," said Laurie, as he handed Jo a saucer of berries.

"Thank you, I prefer spiders," she replied, fishing up two unwary little ones who had gone to a creamy death. "How dare you remind me of that horrid dinner party, when yours is so nice in every way?" added Jo as they both laughed and ate out of one plate, the china having run short.

"I had an uncommonly good time that day, and haven't got over it yet. This is no credit to me, you know, I don't do anything. It's you and Meg and Brooke who make it go, and I'm no end obliged to you. What shall we do when we can't eat any more?" asked Laurie.

"Have games till it's cooler. I brought Authors, and I dare say Miss Kate knows something new and nice. Go and ask her; she's company, and you ought to stay with her more."

"Aren't you company too? I thought she'd suit Brooke, but he keeps talking to Meg, and Kate just stares at them through that ridiculous glass of hers. I'm going."

Miss Kate did know several new games, and as the girls would not, and the boys could not, eat any more, they all adjourned to the oak tree to play rigmarole.

"One person begins a story, any nonsense you like, and tells as long as he pleases, only taking care to stop short at some exciting point, when the next takes it up and does the same. It's very funny when well done, and makes a perfect jumble. Please start it, Mr. Brooke," said Kate.

Lying on the grass at the feet of the two young ladies, Mr. Brooke obediently began the story, with the handsome brown eyes steadily fixed upon the sunshiny river.

"Once upon a time, a knight went out into the world to seek his fortune, for he had nothing but his sword and his shield. He traveled a long while, nearly twenty-eight years, till he came to the palace of a good old king, who had offered a reward to anyone who would train a fine but unbroken colt, of which he was very fond. The knight agreed to try, and the colt was a gallant fellow, and soon learned to love his new master. Every day the knight rode him through the city and as he rode he looked everywhere for a certain beautiful face, which he had seen many times in his dreams, but never found. One day, he saw at the window of a ruinous castle the lovely face. Several captive princesses were kept there by a spell, and spun all day to lay up money to buy their liberty. The knight wished intensely that he could free them, but he was poor. At last he went and knocked; the great door flew open, and he beheld . . ."

"A ravishingly lovely lady, who exclaimed, with a cry of rapture, 'At last! At last!' " continued Kate, who had read French novels, and admired the style. " 'Tis she!' cried Count Gustave, and fell at her feet in an ecstasy of joy. 'Oh, rise!' she said, extending a hand of marble fairness. 'Never! Till you tell me how I may rescue you,' swore the knight, still kneeling. 'Alas, my cruel fate condemns me to remain here till my tyrant is destroyed.' 'Where is the villain?' 'In the mauve salon. Go, brave heart, and save me from despair.' 'I obey, and return victorious or dead!' With these thrilling words he rushed away, and flinging open the door of the mauve salon, was about to enter, when he received . . ."

"A stunning blow from the big Greek lexicon, which an old fellow in a black gown fired at him," said Ned. "Instantly Sir What's-his-name recovered himself, pitched the tyrant out of the window, and turned; found the door locked, tore up the curtains, made a rope ladder, got halfway down when the ladder broke, and he went head first into the moat, sixty feet below. He could swim like a duck, paddled round the castle till he came to a little door guarded by two stout fellows, knocked their heads together till they cracked like a couple of nuts, then, by a trifling exertion of his prodigious strength, he smashed in the door, went up stone steps covered with dust a foot thick, toads as big as your fist, and spiders. At the top of these steps he came plump upon a sight that chilled his blood . . ."

"A tall figure, all in white with a veil over its face and a lamp in its wasted hand," went on Meg. "It beckoned, gliding noiselessly before him down a corridor as dark and cold as any tomb. The ghostly figure ever and anon turned its face toward him, showing the glitter of awful eyes through its white veil. They reached a curtained door, behind which sounded lovely music. He sprang forward to enter, but the specter plucked him back, and waved threateningly before him a . . ."

"Snuffbox," said Jo in a sepulchral tone, which convulsed the audience. " 'Thankee,' said the knight politely, as he took a pinch and sneezed seven times so violently that his head fell off. 'Ha! Ha!' laughed the ghost, and having peeped through the keyhole at the princesses spinning away for dear life, the evil spirit picked up her victim and put him in a large tin box, where there were eleven other knights packed together without their heads, like sardines, who all rose and began to . . ."

"Dance a hornpipe," cut in Fred, as Jo paused for breath, "and, as they danced, the rubbishy old castle turned to a man-of-war in full sail. 'Up with the jib, reef the tops'l halliards, helm hard alee, and man the guns!' roared the captain, as a Portuguese pirate hove in sight, with a flag black as ink flying from her foremast. Of course the British won, they always do."

"No, they don't!" cried Jo, aside.

"Having taken the pirate captain prisoner, 'Bosun's mate, take a bight of the flying-jib sheet, and start this villain if he doesn't confess his sins double quick,' said the British captain. The Portuguese held his tongue and walked the plank, while the jolly tars cheered. But the sly dog dived, came up under the man-of war, scuttled her, and down she went, with all sail set, 'To the bottom of the sea, sea, sea,' where . . ."

"Oh, gracious! What *shall* I say!" cried Sallie, as Fred ended his rigmarole, in which he had jumbled together pell-mell nautical phrases and facts out of one of his favorite books. "Well, a nice mermaid welcomed them. By-and-by a diver came down, and the mermaid said, 'I'll give you this box of pearls if you can take it up.' So the diver hoisted it up, and left it in a great lonely field, where it was found by a . . ."

"Little goosegirl, who kept a hundred fat geese in the field," said Amy. "The little girl was sorry for them, and asked what she should use for new heads, since the old ones were lost, and all the geese opened their hundred mouths and screamed . . ."

" 'Cabbages!' " continued Laurie promptly. "The girl ran to get twelve fine ones from her garden. The knights thanked her, for there were so many cabbage heads in the world that no one thought anything of it. The princesses had spun themselves free and all gone to be married, but one. Mounting his colt, the good knight rushed to the castle. Peeping over the hedge, he saw the last princess picking flowers in her garden. 'Will you give me a rose?' said he. 'You must come and get it. I can't come to you, it isn't proper,' said she, as sweet as honey. He tried to climb over the hedge, but it seemed to grow higher and higher; then he tried to push through, but it grew thicker and thicker.

So he made a little hole through which he peeped, imploring, 'Let me in!' But the pretty princess picked her roses quietly, and left him to fight his way in. Whether he did or not, Frank will tell you."

"I can't. I'm not playing. I never do," said Frank, dismayed at the sentimental predicament out of which he was to rescue the absurd couple. Beth had disappeared behind Jo, and Grace was asleep.

"So the poor knight is to be left sticking in the hedge, is he?" asked Mr. Brooke, still watching the river.

"I guess the princess gave him a posy, and opened the gate after a while," said Laurie, smiling to himself, as he threw acorns at his tutor.

"Do you know Truth?" asked Sallie, after their story.

"I hope so," said Meg soberly.

"The game, I mean!"

"What is it?" said Fred.

"Why, you pile up your hands, choose a number, and draw out your hands, and the person whose hand gets that number has to answer truly any questions put by the rest. It's great fun."

"Let's try it," said Jo, who liked new experiments.

Miss Kate and Mr. Brooke, Meg, and Ned declined, but Fred, Sallie, Jo, and Laurie piled and drew, and the lot fell to Laurie.

"Who are your heroes?" asked Jo.

"Grandfather and Napoleon."

"Which lady here do you think prettiest?" said Sallie.

"Margaret."

"Which do you like best?" from Fred.

"Jo, of course."

"What silly questions you ask!" And Jo gave a disdainful shrug as the rest laughed at Laurie's matter-of-fact tone.

"Try again. Truth isn't a bad game," said Fred.

"It's a good one for you," retorted Jo in a low voice. Her turn came next.

"What is your greatest fault?" asked Fred, by way of testing in her the virtue he lacked himself.

"A quick temper."

"What do you most wish for?" said Laurie.

"A pair of bootlaces," returned Jo, guessing his generous purpose.

"Not a true answer. You must say what you really do want most."

"Genius. Don't you wish you could give it to me, Laurie?" And she slyly smiled in his disappointed face.

"What virtues do you most admire in a man?" asked Sallie.

"Courage and honesty."

"Now my turn," said Fred.

"Let's give it to him," whispered Laurie to Jo, who nodded and asked at once, "Didn't you cheat at croquet?"

"Well, yes, a little bit."

"Good! Didn't you take your story out of *The Sea Lion*?" asked Laurie.

"Rather."

"Don't you think the English nation perfect in every respect?" asked Sallie.

"I should be ashamed of myself if I didn't."

"He's a true John Bull. Now, Miss Sallie, you shall have a chance. I'll ask if you don't think you are something of a flirt," said Laurie, as Jo nodded to Fred as a sign that peace was declared.

"You impertinent boy! Of course I'm not," exclaimed Sallie, with an air that proved the contrary.

"What do you hate most?" asked Fred.

"Spiders and rice pudding."

"What do you like best?" asked Jo.

"Dancing and French gloves."

"Well, I think Truth is silly; let's have a sensible game of Authors," proposed Jo.

Ned, Frank, and the little girls played. Miss Kate took out her sketch again, and Margaret watched her, while Mr. Brooke lay on the grass with a book which he did not read.

"How beautifully you do it! I wish I could draw," said Meg.

"Why don't you learn?" replied Miss Kate graciously.

"I haven't time."

"Your mamma prefers other accomplishments, I fancy. So did mine, but I proved to her that I had talent by taking a few lessons privately, and then she was willing I should go on. Can't you do the same with your governess?"

"I have none."

"I forgot young ladies in America go to school more than with us. Very fine schools they are, too, Papa says. You go to a private one, I suppose?"

"I don't go at all. I am a governess myself."

"Oh, indeed!" said Miss Kate; but she might as well have said, "How dreadful!" Something in her face made Meg wish she had not been so frank.

Mr. Brooke said quickly, "Young ladies in America love independence as much as their ancestors did, and are admired and respected for supporting themselves."

"Oh, yes, of course. We have many most respectable young women who do the same and are employed by the nobility, because, being the daughters of gentlemen, they are well bred, you know," said Miss Kate in a patronizing tone that hurt Meg's pride, and made her work seem degrading.

"Did the German song suit you?" inquired Mr. Brooke, breaking an awkward pause.

"Oh, yes! It was very sweet, and I'm much obliged to whoever translated it for me." Meg's downcast face brightened.

"Don't you read German?" asked Miss Kate with a look of surprise.

"Not very well. My father, who taught me, is away, and I don't get on very fast alone, for I've no one to correct my pronunciation."

Mr. Brooke laid his German edition of Mary Stuart on her lap and invited her to try it, but she was reluctant. Miss Kate offered to read a bit, and did so perfectly correctly but with no expression. When she returned the book to Meg, Mr. Brooke pointed out the passage for Meg to try.

Meg, obediently following the long grass-blade which her new tutor used to point with, read slowly and timidly, making poetry of the hard words with her musical voice. Down the page went the green guide, and presently, Meg read as if alone, giving a little touch of tragedy to the words of the unhappy Mary, Queen of Scots. If she had seen the brown eyes then, she would have stopped short; but she never looked up.

"Very well indeed!" said Mr. Brooke, as she paused, ignoring her many mistakes, and looking as if he did indeed "love to teach."

Miss Kate shut her sketchbook, saying, "You've a nice accent and in time will be a clever reader. I advise you to learn, for German is a valuable accomplishment to teachers. I must look after Grace, she is romping." And Miss Kate strolled away, adding to herself with a shrug, "What odd people these Yankees are. I'm afraid Laurie will be quite ruined by them."

"I forgot that English people turn up their noses at governesses," said Meg, with an annoyed expression.

"Tutors also have a hard time of it there, as I know to my sorrow. There's no place like America for us workers, Miss Margaret." And Mr. Brooke looked contented and cheerful.

"I'm glad I live in it then. I only wish I liked teaching as you do."

"I think you would if you had Laurie for a pupil. I shall be sorry to lose him next year," said Mr. Brooke.

"Going to college, I suppose?" Meg's lips asked that question, but her eyes added, And what becomes of you?

"Yes, it's high time he went, for he is ready; and as soon as he is off, I shall turn soldier. I am needed."

"I should think every young man would want to go, though it is hard for the mothers and sisters who stay at home," she said.

"I have neither, and few friends to care whether I live or die," said Mr. Brooke bitterly.

"Laurie and his grandfather would care a great deal, and we should all be sorry to have any harm happen to you," said Meg heartily.

"Thank you," began Mr. Brooke, looking cheerful again, but before he could finish his speech, Ned, mounted on the old horse, came lumbering up to display his equestrian skill.

"Don't you love to ride?" asked Grace of Amy.

"My sister Meg used to ride when Papa was rich, but we don't keep any horses now, except Ellen Tree," added Amy, laughing.

"Tell me about Ellen Tree. Is it a donkey?" asked Grace curiously.

"Why, you see, Jo is crazy about horses and so am I, but we've only got an old sidesaddle and no horse. Out in our garden is an apple tree that has a nice low branch, so Jo put the saddle on it, fixed some reins on the part that turns up, and we bounce away on Ellen Tree whenever we like."

"How funny!" laughed Grace. "I have a pony at home, and ride nearly every day in the park with Fred and Kate; it's very nice, for my friends go, too, and the Row is full of ladies and gentlemen."

"Dear, how charming! I hope I shall go abroad some day, but I'd rather go to Rome than the Row," said Amy, who had not the remotest idea what the Row was and wouldn't have asked for the world.

Frank pushed his crutch away from him with an impatient gesture. Beth, who was collecting the Author cards, looked up and said, in her shy yet friendly way, "I'm afraid you are tired; can I do anything for you?"

"Talk to me, please. It's dull, sitting by myself," answered Frank, who had evidently been used to being made much of at home.

If he had asked her to deliver a Latin oration, it would not have seemed a more impossible task to bashful Beth; but the poor boy looked so wistfully at her that she bravely resolved to try.

"What do you like to talk about?" she asked, fumbling over the cards and dropping half as she tried to tie them up.

"Well, I like to hear about cricket and boating and hunting."

What shall I do? I don't know anything about them, thought Beth, and forgetting the boy's misfortune in her flurry, she said, hoping to make him talk, "I never saw any hunting, but I suppose you know all about it."

"I did once, but I can never hunt again, for I got hurt leaping a confounded five-barred gate, so there are no more horses and hounds for me" said Frank with a sigh that made Beth hate herself for her innocent blunder.

"Your deer are much prettier than our ugly buffaloes," she said, turning to the prairies for help. Buffaloes proved soothing and satisfactory, and in her eagerness to amuse another, Beth forgot herself.

"I haven't heard Frank laugh so much for ever so long," said Grace to Amy, as they sat discussing dolls and making tea sets out of the acorn cups.

"My sister Beth is a *fastidious* girl, when she likes to be," said Amy, well pleased at Beth's success. She meant "fascinating," but as Grace didn't know the exact meaning of either word, "fastidious" sounded well and made a good impression.

More games finished the afternoon. At sunset the tent was struck, hampers packed, wickets pulled up, boats loaded, and the whole party floated down the river, singing at the tops of their voices. Ned warbled a serenade and looked at Meg with such a sentimental expression that she laughed outright and spoiled his song.

"How can you be so cruel to me?" he whispered. "You've kept close to that starched-up English woman all day, and now you snub me."

"I didn't mean to, but you looked so funny I couldn't help it," replied Meg, passing over the first part of his reproach, for it was true that she *had* shunned him, remembering the Moffat party.

The little party separated with cordial good nights and goodbyes, for the Vaughns were going to Canada. As the four sisters went home through the garden, Miss Kate looked after them, saying, "In spite of their demonstrative manners, American girls are very nice when one knows them."

"I quite agree with you," said Mr. Brooke.

13
CASTLES IN THE AIR

LAURIE LAY LUXURIOUSLY swinging to and fro in his hammock one warm September afternoon, wondering what his neighbors were doing, but too lazy to go and find out. He was wishing he could live the day over again. He had neglected his studies and tried Mr. Brooke's patience. He had displeased his grandfather by playing the piano half the afternoon. He had frightened the maids half out of their wits by hinting that one of his dogs was going mad, and he had scolded the stableman. Then he flung himself into his hammock to fume over the stupidity of the world in general, till the peace of the lovely day quieted him in spite of himself. At last he heard voices.

"What in the world are those girls doing now?" thought Laurie. He could see that each wore a large, flopping hat, a brown linen pouch slung over one shoulder, and carried a long staff. All walked quietly through the garden, out at the little back gate, and began to climb the hill that lay between the house and the river.

"Well, that's not very kind of them," said Laurie to himself, "to have a picnic and never ask me! Perhaps they forgot the boat key. I'll take it to them and see what's going on." He hunted for the key, then took the shortest way to the boathouse, where he waited for them, but no one came, and he went up the hill to look for them. From the heart of a grove of pines came a clearer sound than the drowsy chirp of the crickets.

The sisters sat together in the shady nook, with sun and shadow flickering over them, the aromatic wind lifting their hair and cooling their hot cheeks. Meg sat upon her cushion, sewing daintily and looking as fresh and sweet as a rose in her pink dress among the green. Beth was sorting the cones that lay thick under the hemlock nearby, for she made pretty things of them. Amy was sketching ferns, and Jo was knitting as she read aloud.

"May I come in, please? Or shall I be a bother?" he asked, advancing slowly.

Jo said at once, "Of course you may. We should have asked you before, only we thought you wouldn't care for such a girl's game as this."

"I always like your games, but if Meg doesn't want me, I'll go away."

"I've no objection, if you do something. It's against the rules to be idle here," replied Meg gravely but graciously.

"Much obliged, for it's as dull as the Desert of Sahara down there. Shall I sew, read, cone, draw, or do all at once?" And Laurie sat down with a submissive expression delightful to behold.

"Finish this story while I set my heel," said Jo, handing him the book.

He began, doing his best to prove his gratitude for the favor of an admission into the "Busy Bee Society." The story was not a long one, and when it was finished, he ventured to ask, "Please, ma'am, could I inquire if this highly instructive and charming institution is a new one?"

"Would you tell him?" asked Meg of her sisters.

"He'll laugh," said Amy warningly.

"I give you my word I won't laugh. Tell away, Jo, don't be afraid."

"The idea of being afraid of you! Well, you see we used to play Pilgrim's Progress, and we have been going on with it in earnest, all winter and summer."

"Yes, I know," said Laurie, nodding wisely.

"Who told you?" demanded Jo.

"I did. I wanted to amuse him one night when you were all away, and he was rather dismal. He did like it, so don't scold, Jo," said Beth meekly.

"You can't keep a secret. Never mind, it saves trouble now."

"Go on, please," said Laurie, as Jo became absorbed in her work, looking a trifle displeased.

"Well, we have tried not to waste our holiday, but each has had a task and worked at it with a will. The vacation is nearly over, and we are ever so glad that we didn't dawdle."

"Yes, I should think so." And Laurie thought regretfully of his own idle days.

"Mother likes to have us out-of-doors as much as possible, so we bring our work here and have nice times. For the fun of it we bring our things in these bags, wear the old hats, use poles to climb the hill, and play pilgrims, as we used to do years ago. We call this hill the Delectable Mountain, for we can look far away and see the country where we hope to live some time."

Jo pointed, for through an opening in the wood one could look across the wide, blue river, the meadows on the other side, far over the outskirts of the great city, to the green hills that rose to meet the sky. The sun was low, and the heavens glowed with the splendor of an autumn sunset. Gold and purple clouds lay on the hilltops, and rising high into the ruddy light were silvery white peaks that shone like the airy spires of some Celestial City.

"How beautiful that is!" said Laurie softly.

"We like to watch it, for it is never the same, but always splendid," replied Amy, wishing she could paint it.

"Jo talks about the country where we hope to live sometime—the real country, she means, with pigs and chickens and haymaking. It would be nice, but I wish the beautiful cloud country up there was real, and we could ever go to it," mused Beth.

"There is a lovelier country even than that, where we *shall* go, by-and-by," answered Meg with her sweet voice.

"It seems so long to wait, so hard to do. I want to fly away at once, as those swallows fly, and go in at that splendid gate."

"You'll get there, Beth, sooner or later, no fear of that," said Jo. "I'm the one that will have to fight and work, and climb and wait, and maybe never get in after all."

"You'll have me for company, if that's any comfort," said Laurie. "I shall have to do a deal of traveling before I come in sight of your Celestial City. If I arrive late, you'll say a good word for me, won't you, Beth?"

Beth answered, "I always imagine it is as it is in the picture in the book, where the shining ones stretch out their hands to welcome poor Christian as he comes up from the river."

"Wouldn't it be fun if all the castles in the air which we make could come true, and we could live in them?" said Jo, after a little pause.

"It would be hard to choose," said Laurie, lying flat.

"You'd have to take your favorite one. What is it?" asked Meg.

"After I'd seen as much of the world as I want to, I'd like to settle in Germany and have just as much music as I choose. I'm to be a famous musician myself, and all creation is to rush to hear me. I'm never to be bothered about money or business, but just enjoy myself and live for what I like. That's my favorite castle. What's yours, Meg?"

Margaret said slowly, "I should like a lovely house, full of all sorts of luxurious things—nice food, pretty clothes, handsome furniture, pleasant people, and heaps of money. I am to be mistress of it, and manage it as I like, with plenty of servants, so I never need work a bit. How I should enjoy it! For I wouldn't be idle, but do good, and make everyone love me dearly."

"Why don't you say you'd have a splendid, wise, good husband and some angelic little children? You know your castle wouldn't be perfect without them," said blunt Jo, who scorned romance, except in books.

"You'd have nothing but horses, inkstands, and novels in yours," answered Meg petulantly.

"Wouldn't I, though! I'd have a stable full of Arabian steeds, rooms piled with books, and I'd write out of a magic inkstand, so that my works should be as famous as Laurie's music. I want to do something splendid before I go into my castle—something heroic or wonderful that won't be forgotten after I'm dead. I don't know what, but I'm on the watch for it, and I mean to astonish you all some day. I think I shall write books, and get rich and famous: that would suit me, so that is *my* favorite dream."

"Mine is to stay at home safe with Father and Mother, and help take care of the family," said Beth contentedly.

"Don't you wish for anything else?" asked Laurie.

"Since I have my little piano, I am perfectly satisfied. I only wish we may all keep well and be together, nothing else."

"I have ever so many wishes, but the pet one is to be an artist, and go to Rome, and do fine pictures, and be the best artist in the whole world" was Amy's modest desire.

"We're an ambitious set, aren't we? Every one of us, but Beth, wants to be rich and famous, and gorgeous in every respect. I do wonder if any of us will ever get our wishes," said Laurie, chewing a piece of grass.

"I've got the key to my castle in the air, but whether I can unlock the door remains to be seen," observed Jo mysteriously.

"I've got the key to mine, but I'm not allowed to try it. Hang college!" muttered Laurie with an impatient sigh.

"Here's mine!" And Amy waved her pencil.

"I haven't got any," said Meg forlornly.

"Yes, you have," said Laurie at once.

"Where?"

"In your face."

"Nonsense, that's of no use."

"Wait and see if it doesn't bring you something worth having," replied the boy, laughing.

"If we are all alive ten years hence, let's meet, and see how many of us have got our wishes, or how much nearer we are then than now," said Jo, always ready with a plan.

"Bless me! How old I shall be—twenty-seven!" exclaimed Meg, who felt grown up already, having just reached seventeen.

"Teddy, you and I will be twenty-six, Beth twenty-four, and Amy twenty-two. What a venerable party!" said Jo.

"I hope I shall have done something to be proud of by that time," said Laurie, "but I'm such a lazy dog, I'm afraid I shall 'dawdle,' Jo."

"You need a motive, Mother says; and when you get it, she is sure you'll work splendidly."

"Is she? By Jupiter, I will, if I only get the chance!" cried Laurie, sitting up with sudden energy. "I ought to be satisfied to please Grandfather, and I do try, but it's working against the grain, you see, and comes hard. He wants me to be an India merchant, as he was, and I'd rather be shot. I hate tea and silk and spices, and every sort of rubbish his old ships bring, and I don't care how soon they go to the bottom when I own them. Going to college ought to satisfy him. But he's set, and I've got to do just as he did, unless I break away and please myself, as my father did. If there was anyone left to stay with the old gentleman, I'd do it tomorrow."

Laurie spoke excitedly, and looked ready to carry his threat into execution on the slightest provocation, for he was growing up fast and had a young man's restless longing to try the world for himself.

"I advise you to sail away in one of your ships, and never come home again till you have tried your own way," said Jo, whose imagination was fired by the thought of such a daring exploit.

"That's not right, Jo. You mustn't talk that way, and Laurie mustn't take your bad advice. You should do just what your grandfather wishes," said Meg in her most maternal tone. "Do your best at college, and when he sees that you try to please him, I'm sure he won't be hard or unjust to you. As you say, there is no one else to stay with and love him, and you'd never forgive yourself if you left him without his permission. Don't be dismal or fret, but do your duty and you'll get your reward, like Mr. Brooke."

"What do you know about him?" asked Laurie, grateful for the good advice, but objecting to the lecture and glad to turn the conversation aside.

"Only what your grandpa told us about him—how he took good care of his own mother till she died, and wouldn't go abroad as tutor to some nice person because he wouldn't leave her. And how he provides now for an old woman who nursed his mother, and never tells anyone, but is just as generous and patient and good as he can be."

"So he is!" said Laurie heartily, as Meg paused, looking flushed and earnest with her story. "It's like Grandpa to find out all about him without letting him know, and to tell all his goodness to others, so that they might like him. If ever I do get my wish, you see what I'll do for Brooke."

"Begin to do something now by not plaguing him," said Meg sharply.

"How do you know I do, miss?"

"I can always tell by his face when he goes away. If you have been good, he looks satisfied and walks briskly; if you have plagued him, he's sober and walks slowly, as if he wanted to go back and do his work better."

"Well, I like that! So you keep an account of my good and bad marks in Brooke's face, do you?"

"Please don't be offended. I didn't mean to preach or tell tales or be silly. I only thought Jo was encouraging you in a feeling which you'd be sorry for by-and-by. You are so kind to us, we feel as if you were our brother and say just what we think. Forgive me, I meant it kindly." And Meg offered her hand with a gesture both affectionate and timid.

Ashamed of his momentary irritation, Laurie squeezed the kind little hand, and said frankly, "I'm the one to be forgiven. I'm cross and have been out of sorts all day. I like to have you tell me my faults and be sisterly, so don't mind if I am grumpy sometimes. I thank you all the same."

Bent on showing that he was not offended, he made himself as agreeable as possible—wound cotton for Meg, recited poetry to please Jo, shook down cones for Beth, and helped Amy with her ferns, proving himself a fit person to belong to the "Busy Bee Society." An amiable turtle strolled up from the river, and then the faint sound of a bell warned them that they would just have time to get home to supper.

"May I come again?" asked Laurie.

"Yes, and I'll teach you to knit as the Scotchmen do. There's a demand for socks just now," added Jo, waving hers like a big blue worsted banner as they parted at the gate.

That night, when Beth played to Mr. Laurence in the twilight, Laurie stood in the shadow of the curtain and watched the old man, who sat with his gray head on his hand, thinking tender thoughts of the dead child he had loved so much. The boy said to himself, with the resolve to make the sacrifice cheerfully, "I'll let my castle go, and stay with the dear old gentleman while he needs me, for I am all he has."

Jo wrote busily with her papers spread out upon a trunk . . .

14
SECRETS

Jo was busy in the garret, for the October days began to grow chilly, and the afternoons were short. For two or three hours the sun lay warmly on the high window, while Jo wrote busily with her papers spread out upon a trunk, and Scrabble, the pet rat, promenaded the beams overhead, accompanied by his oldest son, very proud of his whiskers. When the last page was filled, Jo signed her name with a flourish and threw down her pen, exclaiming, "There, I've done my best! If this won't suit I shall have to wait till I can do better."

Lying back on the sofa, she read the manuscript carefully through, making dashes here and there, and putting in many exclamation points, which looked like little balloons. Then she tied it up with a smart red ribbon, and sat a minute looking at it with a sober, wistful expression. From a tin box, she produced another manuscript, and putting both in her pocket, crept quietly downstairs, leaving her friends to nibble her pens and taste her ink.

She put on her hat and jacket as noiselessly as possible, and going to the back entry window, got out upon the roof of a low porch, swung herself down to the grassy bank, and took a roundabout way to the road. Once there, she hailed a passing bus and rolled away to town, looking merry and mysterious. If anyone had been watching her, he would have thought her movements decidedly peculiar, for on alighting, she hurried till she reached a certain address, went into the doorway, looked up the dirty stairs, and after standing stock still a minute, suddenly walked away as rapidly as she came. This maneuver she repeated several times, to the great amusement of a black-eyed young gentleman watching her from a window. On returning for the third time, Jo gave herself a shake, pulled her hat over her eyes, and walked up the stairs, looking as if she were going to have all her teeth out.

There was a dentist's sign, among others, which adorned the entrance, and after staring a moment at the pair of artificial jaws which slowly opened and shut to draw attention to a fine set of teeth, the young gentleman posted himself in the opposite doorway, saying with a smile and a shiver, "It's like her to come alone, but if she has a bad time she'll need someone to help her home."

In ten minutes Jo came running downstairs with a red face and the general appearance of a person who had just passed through a trying ordeal of some sort. When she saw the young gentleman she looked anything but pleased, and passed him with a nod. He followed her, asking with an air of sympathy, "Did you have a bad time?"

"Not very."

"Why did you go alone?"

"I didn't want anyone to know."

"How many did you have out?"

Jo looked at her friend as if she did not understand him, then began to laugh as if mightily amused at something. "There are two which I want to have come out, but I must wait a week."

"What are you laughing at? You are up to some mischief, Jo," said Laurie, looking mystified.

"So are you. What were you doing, sir, up in that pool hall?"

"Begging your pardon, ma'am, it wasn't a pool hall, but a gymnasium, and I was taking a lesson in fencing."

"I'm glad of that."

"Why?"

"You can teach me, and then when we play *Hamlet*, you can be Laertes, and we'll make a fine thing of the fencing scene. I'm glad that you were not in the pool hall, because I hope you never go to such places. Do you?"

"Not often."

"I wish you wouldn't."

"It's no harm, Jo. I have billiards at home, but it's no fun unless you have good players. So, as I'm fond of it, I come sometimes and have a game with Ned Moffat or some of the other fellows."

"Oh dear, you'll get to liking it better and better, and will waste time and money, and grow like those dreadful boys. I did hope you'd stay respectable," said Jo, shaking her head.

"Can't a fellow take a little innocent amusement now and then without losing his respectability?" asked Laurie.

"That depends upon how and where he takes it. I don't like Ned and his set, and wish you'd keep out of it. Mother won't let us have him at our house, though he wants to come. She can't bear fashionable young men, and she'd shut us all up in bandboxes rather than have us associate with them."

"Well, she needn't get out her bandboxes yet. I'm not a fashionable party and don't mean to be, but I do like harmless larks now and then."

"Lark away, but don't get wild, will you? Or there will be an end to all our good times."

"I'll be a double-distilled saint."

"I can't bear saints. Just be a simple, honest, respectable boy, and we'll never desert you. I don't know what I should do if you acted like Mr. King's son. He had plenty of money, but didn't know how to spend it, and got tipsy and gambled, and ran away, and forged his father's name, I believe, and was altogether horrid."

"You think I'm likely to do the same? Much obliged."

"No, I don't—oh, dear, no! But I hear people talking about money being such a temptation, and I sometimes wish you were poor. I shouldn't worry then."

"Do you worry about me, Jo?"

"A little, when you look moody or discontented, as you sometimes do. You have such a strong will, if you once get started wrong, I'm afraid it would be hard to stop you."

Laurie walked in silence a few minutes. "If you are going to deliver lectures all the way home, I'll take a bus; if you are not, I'd like to walk with you and tell you something very interesting. It's a secret, and if I tell you, you must tell me yours."

"I haven't got any," began Jo, but stopped suddenly, remembering that she had.

"You know you have. You can't hide anything, so up and fess, or I won't tell," cried Laurie.

"You won't tease me?"

"I never tease."

"Yes, you do. You get everything you want out of people. I don't know how you do it, but you are a born wheedler."

"Thank you. Fire away."

"Well, I've left two stories with a newspaperman, and he's to give his answer next week," whispered Jo, in his ear.

"Hurrah for Miss March, the celebrated American authoress!" cried Laurie, throwing up his hat and catching it again, to the great delight of two ducks, four cats, five hens, and half a dozen Irish children, for they were out of the city now.

"Hush! It won't come to anything, I dare say, but I couldn't rest till I had tried, and I said nothing about it because I didn't want anyone else to be disappointed."

"It won't fail. Why, Jo, your stories are works of Shakespeare compared to half the rubbish that is published every day. Won't it be fun to see them in print, and shan't we feel proud of our authoress?"

Jo's eyes sparkled, for it is always pleasant to be believed in, and a friend's praise is always sweetest.

"Where's *your* secret? Play fair, Teddy," she said.

"I may get into a scrape for telling, but I didn't promise not to, so I will, for I never feel easy in my mind till I've told you any plummy bit of news. I know where Meg's glove is."

"Is that all?" said Jo, looking disappointed, as Laurie nodded and twinkled with a face full of mysterious intelligence.

Laurie bent, and whispered three words in Jo's ear. She stood and stared at him for a minute, looking both surprised and displeased, then walked on, saying sharply, "How do you know?"

"Saw it."

"Where?"

"Pocket."

"All this time?"

"Yes, isn't that romantic?"

"No, it's horrid."

"Don't you like it?"

"Of course I don't. It's ridiculous. What would Meg say?"

"You are not to tell anyone. Mind that."

"Well, I won't for the present, anyway, but I'm disgusted, and wish you hadn't told me."

"I thought you'd be pleased."

"At the idea of anybody coming to take Meg away? No, thank you."

"You'll feel better about it when somebody comes to take you away."

"I'd like to see anyone try it," cried Jo fiercely.

"So should I!" And Laurie chuckled at the idea.

"I don't think secrets agree with me, I feel rumpled up in my mind since you told me that," said Jo ungratefully.

"Race me down this hill, and you'll be all right," suggested Laurie.

No one was in sight, the smooth road sloped invitingly before her, and Jo darted away, soon leaving her hat behind her and scattering hairpins as she ran. Laurie reached the goal first and was satisfied with the success of his treatment, for Jo came panting up with flying hair, bright eyes, ruddy cheeks, and no signs of dissatisfaction in her face.

"I wish I was a horse, then I could run for miles in this splendid air, and not lose my breath. Go, pick up my things, like the cherub you are," said Jo, dropping down under a maple tree, which was carpeting the bank with crimson leaves.

Laurie departed, and Jo bundled up her braids, hoping no one would pass by till she was tidy again. But someone did pass, and who should it be but Meg, looking particularly ladylike, for she had been making calls.

"What in the world are you doing here?" she asked, regarding her disheveled sister with well-bred surprise.

"Getting leaves," meekly answered Jo, sorting the rosy handful she had just swept up.

"And hairpins," added Laurie, throwing half a dozen into Jo's lap. "They grow on this road, Meg; so do brown straw hats."

"You have been running, Jo. When *will* you stop romping?" said Meg reprovingly, as she settled her cuffs and smoothed her hair, with which the wind had taken liberties.

"Never till I'm stiff and old and have to use a crutch. Don't try to make me grow up before my time, Meg. It's hard enough to have you change all of a sudden. Let me be a little girl as long as I can."

As she spoke, Jo bent over the leaves to hide the trembling of her lips, for Laurie's secret made her dread the separation which must surely come sometime. He saw the trouble in her face and drew Meg's attention from it by asking quickly, "Where have you been calling, all so fine?"

"At the Gardiners, and Sallie has been telling me all about Belle Moffat's wedding. It was splendid, and they have gone to spend the winter in Paris."

"Do you envy her, Meg?" said Laurie.

"I'm afraid I do."

"I'm glad of it!" muttered Jo, tying on her hat with a jerk. "Because if you care much about riches, you will never go and marry a poor man."

"I shall never '*go* and marry' anyone," observed Meg, walking on with great dignity while the others followed, laughing, whispering, skipping stones, and "behaving like children," as Meg said to herself, though she might have been tempted to join them if she had not had her best dress on.

For a week or two, Jo behaved strangely. She rushed to the door when the postman rang, was rude to Mr. Brooke whenever they met, and would sit looking at Meg with a woebegone face. Laurie and she were always making signs to one another. On the second Saturday, Meg, as she sat sewing at her window, was scandalized by the sight of Laurie chasing Jo all over the garden and finally capturing her in Amy's bower. What went on there, Meg could not see, but shrieks of laughter were heard, followed by the murmur of voices and a great flapping of newspapers.

"What shall we do with that girl? She never *will* behave like a young lady," sighed Meg.

"I hope she won't. She is so funny and dear as she is," said Beth, who never betrayed that she was a little hurt at Jo's having secrets from her.

In a few minutes Jo bounced in, laid herself on the sofa, and pretended to read.

"Have you anything interesting there?" asked Meg with disdain.

"Nothing but a story. Won't amount to much, I guess," returned Jo, carefully keeping the name of the paper out of sight.

"You'd better read it aloud. That will amuse us and keep you out of mischief," said Amy in her most grown-up tone.

"What's the name?" asked Beth, wondering why Jo kept her face behind the sheet.

"The Rival Painters." With a loud "Hem!" and a long breath, Jo began to read fast. The girls listened with interest, for the tale was romantic, and somewhat pathetic, as most of the characters died in the end.

"I like that about the splendid picture" was Amy's approving remark when Jo finished.

"I prefer the lovering part. Viola and Angelo are two of our favorite names—isn't that odd?" said Meg, wiping her eyes.

"Who wrote it?" asked Beth, who had caught a glimpse of Jo's face.

The reader suddenly sat up, cast away the paper, displaying a flushed countenance, and with a funny mixture of solemnity and excitement replied in a loud voice, "Your sister."

"You?" cried Meg, dropping her work.

"It's very good," said Amy critically.

"I knew it! I knew it! Oh, my Jo, I am so proud!" Beth ran to hug her sister and exult over this splendid success.

Meg wouldn't believe it till she saw the words, "Miss Josephine March," actually printed in the paper. Amy offered hints for a sequel, which unfortunately couldn't be carried out, as the hero and heroine were dead. Beth got excited, and skipped and sang with joy. Hannah came in to exclaim, "Sakes alive, well I never!" in great astonishment. Mrs. March was proud. Jo laughed, with tears in her eyes, as she declared she might as well be a peacock and be done with it. The paper passed from hand to hand.

"Tell us all about it." "When did it come?" "How much did you get for it?" "What *will* Father say?" "Won't Laurie laugh?" cried the family, all in one breath as they clustered about Jo, for these foolish, affectionate people made a jubilee of every little household joy.

"Stop jabbering, girls, and I'll tell you everything," said Jo. Having told how she disposed of her tales, she added, "And when I went to get my answer, the man said he liked them both, but didn't pay beginners, only let them print in his paper. It was good practice, he said, and when the beginners improved, anyone would pay. So I let him have the two stories, and today this was sent to me, and Laurie caught me with it and insisted on seeing it, so I let him. He said it was good, and I shall write more, and he's going to get the next paid for, and I *am* so happy, for in time I may be able to support myself and help the girls."

Jo's breath gave out here, and wrapping her head in the paper, she bedewed her little story with a few tears, for to be independent and earn the praise of those she loved were the dearest wishes of her heart.

15
A TELEGRAM

"NOVEMBER IS THE MOST DISAGREEABLE MONTH in the whole year," said Margaret, standing at the window one dull afternoon, looking out at the frostbitten garden.

"That's the reason I was born in it," observed Jo pensively, unaware of the smudge on her nose.

"If something pleasant should happen now, we should think it a delightful month," said Beth, who took a hopeful view of everything, even November.

"I dare say, but nothing pleasant ever does happen in this family," said Meg, who was out of sorts. "We go grubbing along day after day, without a bit of change, and little fun. We might as well be on a treadmill."

"How blue we are!" cried Jo. "You see other girls having splendid times, while you grind, grind, year in and year out. Oh, don't I wish I could manage things for you as I do for my heroines! I'd have some rich relation leave you a fortune unexpectedly. Then you'd dash out as an heiress, scorn everyone who has slighted you, go abroad, and come home my Lady Something in a blaze of splendor and elegance."

"People don't have fortunes left to them in that style nowadays, men have to work and women to marry for money. It's a dreadfully unjust world," said Meg bitterly.

"Jo and I are going to make fortunes for you all. Just wait ten years and see if we don't," said Amy, who sat in a corner making little clay models of birds, fruit, and faces.

"I can't wait, and I'm afraid I haven't much faith in ink and dirt, though I'm grateful for your good intentions," Meg sighed, and turned to the frostbitten garden again.

Beth, who sat at the other window, said, smiling, "Two pleasant things are going to happen right away. Marmee is coming down the street, and Laurie is tramping through the garden as if he has something nice to tell."

In they both came, Mrs. March with her usual question, "Any letter from Father, girls?" and Laurie to say in his persuasive way, "Won't some of you come for a drive? It's a dull day, but the air isn't bad, and I'm going to take Brooke home. Come, Jo, you will go, won't you?"

"We will be ready in a minute," cried Amy, running away to wash her hands.

"Can I do anything for you, Madam Mother?" asked Laurie, leaning over Mrs. March's chair with the affectionate look and tone he always gave her.

A sharp ring interrupted them, and a minute later Hannah came in with a letter. "It's one of them horrid telegraph things, mum," she said, handling it as if she was afraid it would explode and do some damage.

At the word "telegraph," Mrs. March snatched it, read the two lines it contained, and dropped back into her chair as white as if the little paper had sent a bullet to her heart. Jo read aloud, in a frightened voice,

Mrs. March:
Your husband is very ill. Come at once.

S. Hale,
Blank Hospital, Washington.

How still the room was as they listened breathlessly, how strangely the day darkened outside, and how suddenly the whole world seemed to change, as if all the happiness and support of their lives was about to be taken from them. Mrs. March stretched out her arms to her daughters, saying, in a tone they never forgot, "I shall go at once, but it may be too late. Oh, children, children, help me to bear it!"

For several minutes there was nothing but the sound of sobbing in the room, mingled with broken words of comfort, tender assurances of help, and hopeful whispers that died away in tears. Poor Hannah was the first to recover, and she set all the rest a good example, for, with her, work was the cure for most afflictions.

"The Lord keep the dear man! I won't waste no time a-cryin', but git your things ready right away, mum," she said heartily, as she wiped her face on her apron, gave her mistress a warm squeeze of the hand with her own hard one, and went away to work like three women in one.

"She's right, there's no time for tears now. Be calm, girls, and let me think." They tried to be calm, poor things, as their mother sat up, looking pale but steady.

"Where's Laurie?" she asked, when she had collected her thoughts and decided on the first duties to be done.

"Here, ma'am. Oh, let me do something!" cried the boy.

"Send a telegram saying I will come at once. The next train goes early in the morning. I'll take that."

"What else? The horses are ready. I can go anywhere, do anything," he said, looking ready to fly to the ends of the earth.

"Leave a note at Aunt March's. Jo, give me that pen and paper." She wrote a note asking to borrow money for her trip. "Now go, but don't kill yourself driving at a desperate pace. There's no need of that." The warning was evidently thrown away, for five minutes later Laurie tore by the window on his own fleet horse, riding as if for his life.

"Jo, run and tell Mrs. King that I can't come. Amy, tell Hannah to get down the black trunk. And Meg and Beth, come and help me find my things, for I'm half bewildered." Everyone scattered like leaves before a gust of wind, and the quiet, happy household was broken up as suddenly as if the paper had been an evil spell.

Mr. Laurence came right away, with friendliest promises of protection for the girls during the mother's absence. He knit his heavy eyebrows, rubbed his hands, and marched abruptly away, saying he'd be back directly. No one had time to think of him again till, as Meg ran through the entry, she came suddenly upon Mr. Brooke.

"I'm sorry to hear of this, Miss March," he said, in his kind, quiet tone. "I came to offer myself as escort to your mother. Mr. Laurence has tasks for me in Washington, and it will give me real satisfaction to be of service to her there."

"How kind you all are! Mother will accept, I'm sure, and it will be such a relief to know that she has someone to take care of her. Thank you very, very much!"

Everything was arranged by the time Laurie returned with a note from Aunt March, enclosing the desired sum, and a few lines repeating what she had often said before—that it was absurd for March to go into the army, that no good would come of it, and she hoped they would take her advice next time. Mrs. March put the note in the fire, the money in her purse, and went on with her preparations, with her lips pressed tightly in a way Jo would have understood if she had been there.

The short afternoon wore away, but still Jo did not come. They began to get anxious, and Laurie went off to find her. He missed her, however, and she came walking in with a peculiar expression full of fun and fear which puzzled the family as much as the roll of bills she laid before her mother, saying with a little choke in her voice, "That's my contribution toward making Father comfortable and bringing him home!"

"My dear, where did you get it? Twenty-five dollars! Jo, I hope you haven't done anything rash!"

"No, it's mine honestly. I didn't beg, borrow, or steal it. I earned it, and I don't think you'll blame me, for I only sold what was my own."

As she spoke, Jo took off her bonnet, and a general outcry arose, for all her abundant hair was cut short.

"Your hair! Your beautiful hair!" "Oh, Jo, how could you? Your one beauty." "My dear girl, there was no need of this." "She doesn't look like my Jo any more, but I love her dearly for it!"

As everyone exclaimed, and Beth hugged the cropped head tenderly, Jo assumed an indifferent air, which did not deceive anyone a particle, and said, rumpling up the brown bob and trying to look as if she liked it, "It doesn't affect the fate of the nation, so don't wail, Beth. It will be good for my vanity. It will do my brains good to have that mop taken off. My head feels deliciously light and cool, and the barber said I could soon have a curly crop, which will be boyish, becoming, and easy to keep in order. I'm satisfied, so please take the money and let's have supper."

"Tell me all about it, Jo. But, my dear, it was not necessary, and I'm afraid you will regret it one of these days," said Mrs. March.

"No, I won't!" returned Jo stoutly, feeling much relieved that her prank was not entirely condemned.

"What made you do it?" asked Amy, who would as soon have thought of cutting off her head as her pretty hair.

"Well, I was wild to do something for Father," replied Jo, as they gathered about the table, for healthy young people can eat even in the midst of trouble. "Meg gave all her quarterly salary toward the rent, and I only got some clothes with mine, so I felt wicked and was determined to have some money if it meant selling the nose off my face to get it."

"You needn't feel wicked, my child: you had no winter things and got the simplest with your own hard earnings," said Mrs. March with a look that warmed Jo's heart.

"I hadn't the least idea of selling my hair at first, but as I went along I kept thinking what I could do. In a barber's window I saw tails of hair with the prices marked, and one black tail, not so thick as mine, was forty dollars. It came over me all of a sudden that I had one thing to make money out of, and without stopping to think, I walked in, asked if they bought hair, and what they would give for mine."

"I don't see how you dared to do it," said Beth in a tone of awe.

"Oh, he was a little man who rather stared at first, as if he wasn't used to having girls bounce into his shop and ask him to buy their hair. He said mine wasn't the fashionable color, and he never paid much for it in the first place—the work put into it made it expensive, and so on. It was getting late, and you know when I start to do a thing, I hate to give it up. So I begged him to take it, and told him why I was in such a hurry. I got excited, and told the story in my topsy-turvy way, and his wife heard, and said so kindly, 'Take it, Thomas, and oblige the young lady. I'd do as much for our Jimmy any day if I had a spire of hair worth selling.' "

"Who was Jimmy?" asked Amy, who liked to have things explained as they went along.

"Her son, she said, who was in the army. How friendly such things make strangers feel, don't they? She talked away all the time the man clipped, and diverted my mind nicely."

"Didn't you feel dreadfully when the first cut came?" asked Meg, with a shiver.

"I took a last look at my hair while the man got his things, and that was the end of it. I will confess, though, I felt odd when I saw the dear old hair laid out on the table, and felt only the short, rough ends of my head. It almost seemed as if I had an arm or a leg cut off. The woman saw me look at it, and picked out a long lock for me to keep. I'll give it to you, Marmee, just to remember past glories by."

Mrs. March folded the wavy chestnut lock, and laid it in her desk. She only said, "Thank you, deary," but something in her face made the girls change the subject, and talk as cheerfully as they could about

Mr. Brooke's kindness and the happy times they would have when Father came home to be nursed.

No one wanted to go to bed when at ten o'clock Mrs. March said, "Come, girls." Beth went to the piano and played the father's favorite hymn. All began singing bravely, but broke down one by one till Beth was left alone, singing with all her heart.

"Go to bed and don't talk, for we must be up early and shall need all the sleep we can get. Good night, my darlings," said Mrs. March, as the hymn ended, for no one cared to try another.

They kissed her quietly, and went to bed silently. Beth and Amy soon fell asleep in spite of the great trouble, but Meg lay awake, thinking the most serious thoughts she had ever known in her short life. Jo lay motionless, and her sister fancied that she was asleep, till a stifled sob made her exclaim, as she touched a wet cheek, "Jo, dear, what is it? Are you crying about Father?"

"No, not now."

"What then?"

"My . . . my hair!" burst out poor Jo. "I'm not sorry. I'd do it again tomorrow, if I could. It's only the vain, selfish part of me that goes and cries in this silly way. Don't tell anyone, it's all over now. I thought you were asleep."

"I can't sleep, I'm so anxious," said Meg.

"Think about something pleasant, and you'll soon drop off."

"I tried it, but felt wider awake than ever."

"What did you think of?"

"Handsome faces—eyes particularly," answered Meg, smiling to herself in the dark.

"What color do you like best?"

"Brown—that is, sometimes. Blue are lovely."

Jo laughed, and Meg sharply ordered her not to talk, then amiably promised to make her hair curl, and fell asleep to dream of living in her castle in the air.

The clocks were striking midnight and the rooms were still as a figure glided quietly from bed to bed, smoothing a coverlet here, settling a pillow there, and pausing to look long and tenderly at each unconscious face, to kiss each with lips that mutely blessed, and to pray the fervent prayers which only mothers utter. As she lifted the curtain to look out into the dreary night, the moon broke suddenly from behind the clouds and shone upon her like a bright, benign face, which seemed to whisper in the silence, "Be comforted, dear soul! There is always light behind the clouds."

16
LETTERS

IN THE COLD GRAY DAWN the sisters lit their lamp and read their chapter with an earnestness never felt before, for now that the shadow of a real trouble had come, the little books were full of help and comfort. As they dressed, they agreed to say goodbye cheerfully and hopefully, without tears or complaints.

Everything seemed strange when they went down—so dim and still outside. Breakfast at that early hour seemed odd, and even Hannah's familiar face looked unnatural as she flew about her kitchen with her nightcap on. The big trunk stood ready in the hall, Mother's cloak and bonnet lay on the sofa, and Mother herself sat trying to eat, but looking so pale and worn that the girls found it hard to keep their resolution. Meg's eyes kept filling in spite of herself, Jo was obliged to hide her face in the kitchen towel more than once, and the little girls wore a grave, troubled expression, as if sorrow was a new experience to them.

Nobody talked much, but as the time drew near and they sat waiting for the carriage, Mrs. March said to the girls, who were all busied about her, one folding her shawl, another smoothing out the strings of her bonnet, a third putting on her overshoes, and a fourth fastening up her traveling bag, "Children, I leave you to Hannah's care and Mr. Laurence's protection. I have no fears for you, yet I am anxious that you should take this trouble rightly. Don't grieve and fret when I am gone. Hope and keep busy, and whatever happens, remember that you never can be fatherless."

"Yes, Mother."

"Meg, dear, watch over your sisters, consult Hannah, and, in any perplexity, go to Mr. Laurence. Be patient, Jo, don't get despondent or do rash things. Write to me often, and be my brave girl. Beth, comfort yourself with your music, and be faithful to the little home duties. And you, Amy, help all you can, be obedient, and keep happy and safe at home."

"We will, Mother! We will!"

They sent loving messages to Father, remembering, as they spoke, that it might be too late to deliver them. They kissed their mother quietly and clung about her tenderly. Laurie and his grandfather came over to see her off, and Mr. Brooke looked so strong and sensible and kind that the girls christened him "Mr. Greatheart" on the spot.

"Goodbye, my darlings! God bless and keep us all!" whispered Mrs. March, as she kissed one dear face after the other, and hurried into the carriage.

As she rolled away, the sun came out, and looking back, she saw it shining on the group at the gate like a good omen. They saw it also, and smiled and waved their hands. The last thing she beheld as she turned the corner was the four bright faces, and behind them like a bodyguard old Mr. Laurence, faithful Hannah, and devoted Laurie.

"How kind everyone is to us!" she said.

"I don't see how they can help it," returned Mr. Brooke, laughing so infectiously that Mrs. March could not help smiling. And so the long journey began with the good omens of sunshine, smiles, and cheerful words.

"I feel as if there had been an earthquake," said Jo.

"It seems as if half the house was gone," added Meg forlornly.

Beth opened her lips to say something, but could only point to the pile of nicely mended hose which lay on Mother's table, showing that even in her last hurried moments she had thought and worked for them. It was a little thing, but it went straight to their hearts, and in spite of their brave resolutions, they all broke down and cried bitterly.

When the shower showed signs of clearing up, Hannah came to the rescue, armed with a coffeepot.

"Now, my dear young ladies, remember what your ma said, and don't fret. Come and have a cup of coffee all round, and then let's fall to work and be a credit to the family." No one could resist her persuasive nods, or the fragrant invitation issuing from the nose of the coffeepot. They drew up to the table, and in ten minutes were all right again.

" 'Hope and keep busy,' that's the motto for us, so let's see who will remember it best. I shall go to Aunt March, as usual. Oh, won't she lecture though!" said Jo, as she sipped with returning spirit.

"I shall go to my Kings, though I'd much rather stay at home and attend to things here," said Meg, wishing she hadn't made her eyes so red.

"No need of that. Beth and I can keep house perfectly well," put in Amy, with an important air.

"Hannah will tell us what to do, and we'll have everything nice when you come home," added Beth, getting out her mop and dish tub without delay.

"I think anxiety is very interesting," observed Amy, eating sugar pensively.

The girls couldn't help laughing, and felt better for it, though Meg shook her head at the young lady who could find consolation in a sugar bowl.

When Jo and Meg left for work, they looked sorrowfully back at the window where they were accustomed to see their mother's face. It was gone, but Beth had remembered the little household ceremony, and there she was, nodding away at them.

"That's so like my Beth!" said Jo, waving her hat, with a grateful face. And away she went, feeling like a shorn sheep on a wintry day.

News about their father comforted the girls very much, for though he was dangerously ill, the daily bulletins from Mr. Brooke grew more and more cheering as the week passed. At first, everyone was eager to write, and plump envelopes were carefully poked into the letter box by one or other of the sisters. One of these packets included the following letters:

My Dearest Mother,

It is impossible to tell you how happy your last letter made us, for the news was so good we couldn't help laughing and crying over it. How very kind Mr. Brooke is, and how fortunate that Mr. Laurence's business detains him near you so long, since he is so useful to you and Father. The girls are as good as gold. Jo helps me with the sewing, and insists on doing all sorts of hard jobs. Beth is as regular about her tasks as a clock, and never forgets what you told her. She grieves about Father, and looks sober except when she is at her little piano. Amy minds me nicely. She does her own hair, and I am teaching her to make buttonholes and mend her stockings. She tries hard, and I know you will be pleased with her improvement. Mr. Laurence watches over us like a motherly old hen, as Jo says, and Laurie is very kind. He and Jo keep us merry, for we get pretty blue sometimes, and feel like orphans, with you so far away. Hannah is a perfect saint. We are all well and busy, but we long, day and night, to have you back. Give my dearest love to Father, and believe me, ever your own

Meg

This note, prettily written on scented paper, was a great contrast to the next, which was scribbled on a big sheet of thin foreign paper, ornamented with blots and all manner of flourishes and curly-tailed letters:

My Precious Marmee,

Three cheers for dear Father! Brooke was a trump to telegraph right off, and let us know the minute he was better. I tried to thank God for being so good to us, but I could only cry, and say, "I'm glad! I'm glad!" Didn't that do as well as a regular prayer? For I felt a great many in my heart. Everyone is so desperately good, it's like living in a nest of turtledoves. Oh, I must tell you that I came near having a quarrel with Laurie. I was right, but didn't speak as I ought, and he marched home, saying he wouldn't come again till I begged pardon. I declared I wouldn't and got mad. It lasted all day. Laurie and I are both so proud, it's hard to beg pardon, but I thought he'd come to it, for I was in the right. He didn't come, and just at night I remembered what you said when Amy fell into the river. I read my little book, felt better, resolved not to let the sun set on my anger, and ran over to tell Laurie I was sorry. I met him at the gate, coming for the same thing. We both laughed, begged each other's pardon, and felt all good and comfortable again.

I made a "pome" yesterday, when I was helping Hannah wash, and as Father likes my silly things, I put in the first half to amuse him. Give him the lovingest hug that ever was, and kiss yourself a dozen times for your

Topsy-Turvy Jo

A SONG FROM THE SUDS

Queen of the tub, I merrily sing,
    While the white foam rises high;
And sturdily wash and rinse and wring,
    And fasten the clothes to dry;

Then out in the free fresh air they swing,
　　Under the sunny sky.
I wish we could wash from our hearts and souls
　　The stains of the week away,
And let water and air by their magic make
　　Ourselves as pure as they;
Then on the earth there would be indeed
　　A glorious washing-day!

Dear Mother,

There is only room for me to send my love, and some pressed pansies for Father to see. I read every morning, try to be good all day, and sing myself to sleep with Father's tune. Everyone is very kind, and we are as happy as we can be without you. Amy wants the rest of the page, so I must stop. I didn't forget to cover the holders, and I wind the clock and air the rooms every day. Kiss dear Father on the cheek. Oh, do come soon to your loving

Little Beth

Ma Chere Mamma,

We are all well I do my lessons always and never correborate the girls—Meg says I mean "contradick" so I put in both words and you can take the properest. Meg is a great comfort to me and lets me have jelly every night at tea its so good for me Jo says because it keeps me sweet tempered. Laurie is not as respeckful as he ought to be now I am almost in my teens, he calls me Chick and talks French to me very fast when I say Merci or Bon jour. The sleeves of my blue dress were all worn out, and Meg put in new ones, but they are more blue than the dress. I felt bad but did not fret. I bear my troubles well but I do wish Hannah would put more starch in my aprons and have buckwheats every day. Can't she? Didn't I make that interrigation point nice? Meg says my punchtuation and spelling are disgraceful and I am mortified but dear me I have so many things to do, I can't stop. Adieu, I send heaps of love to Papa.

Your affectionate daughter,
Amy Curtis March

Dear Mis March,

I jes drop a line to say we get along fust rate. The girls is clever and fly around right smart. Jo done out a tub of clothes on Monday, but she starched em afore they was wrenched, and blued a pink calico dress till I thought I should a died a laughin. I don't let the girls hev coffee only once a week, accordin to your wish, and keep em on plain wholesome vittles. Amy does well about frettin, wearing her best clothes and eatin sweet stuff. Mr. Laurie heartens up the girls, and so I let em hev full swing. The old gentleman sends heaps of things, and is rather wearin, but means wal, and it aint my place to say nothin. My bread is riz, so no more at this time. I send my duty to Mr. March and hope he's seen the last of his Pewmonia.

Yours Respectful,
Hannah Mullet

Head Nurse of Ward No.2,

A salute of twenty-four guns was fired on receipt of good news from Washington, and a dress parade took place at headquarters.

Colonel Teddy

Dear Madam,

The little girls are all well. Beth and my boy report daily. Hannah is a model servant, and guards pretty Meg like a dragon. Glad the fine weather holds. Pray make Brooke useful, and draw on me for funds if expenses exceed your estimate. Don't let your husband go without anything. Thank God he is mending.

Your sincere friend and servant,
James Laurence

17
LITTLE FAITHFUL

FOR A WEEK THE AMOUNT OF VIRTUE in the old house would have supplied the neighborhood. It was really amazing, for everyone seemed in a heavenly frame of mind, and self-denial was all the fashion. But when relieved of their first anxiety about their father, the girls relaxed their praiseworthy efforts for a little, and began to fall back into the old ways.

Jo caught a bad cold through neglect to cover her shorn head and was ordered to stay at home till she was better, for Aunt March didn't like to hear people read with colds in their heads. Amy found that housework and art did not go well together, and returned to her clay. Meg went daily to her pupils, and sewed, or thought she did, at home, but much time was spent reading the letters from Washington over and over. Beth kept on, with only slight relapses into idleness or grieving.

She did all her little duties faithfully each day, and many of her sisters' also, for they were forgetful. When her heart got heavy with longings for Mother or fears for Father, she went away into a certain closet, hid her face in the folds of a certain dear old gown, and prayed her little prayer quietly by herself. Nobody knew what cheered her up, but everyone felt how sweet and helpful Beth was, and went to her for comfort or advice in their small affairs.

This experience was a test of character, and when the first excitement was over, they felt that they had done well and deserved praise. So they did, but their mistake was in ceasing to do well.

"Meg, I wish you'd go and see the Hummels. You know Mother told us not to forget them," said Beth, ten days after Mrs. March's departure.

"I'm too tired to go this afternoon," replied Meg, rocking comfortably as she sewed.

"Can't you, Jo?" asked Beth.

"Too stormy for me with my cold."

"I thought it was almost well."

"It's well enough for me to go out with Laurie, but not well enough to go to the Hummels'," said Jo, laughing, but looking a little ashamed.

"Why don't you go yourself?" asked Meg.

"I *have* been every day, but the baby is sick, and I don't know what to do for it. Mrs. Hummel goes away to work, and Lottchen takes care of it. But it gets sicker and sicker, and I think you or Hannah ought to go."

Beth spoke earnestly, and Meg promised she would go tomorrow.

"Ask Hannah for some food to take, Beth. The air will do you good," said Jo, adding apologetically, "I'd go, but I want to finish my writing."

"My head aches and I'm tired, so I thought maybe some of you would go," said Beth.

"Amy will be in presently, and she will run down for us," suggested Meg.

"Well, I'll rest a little and wait for her."

So Beth lay down on the sofa, the others returned to their work, and the Hummels were forgotten. An hour passed. Amy did not come, Meg went to her room to try on a new dress, Jo was absorbed in her story, and Hannah was sound asleep before the kitchen fire, when Beth quietly put on her hood, filled her basket with odds and ends, and went out into the chilly air with a grieved look in her patient eyes. It was late when she came back, and no one saw her creep upstairs and shut herself into her mother's room. Half an hour later, Jo went in for something, and there found Beth sitting on the medicine chest, with red eyes and a camphor-bottle in her hand.

"Christopher Columbus! What's the matter?" cried Jo, as Beth put out her hand as if to warn her off, and asked quickly, "You've had the scarlet fever, haven't you?"

"Years ago, when Meg did. Why?"

"Then I'll tell you. Oh, Jo, the baby's dead!"

"What baby?"

"Mrs. Hummel's. It died in my lap before she got home," cried Beth with a sob.

"My poor dear, how dreadful for you! I ought to have gone," said Jo, taking her sister in her arms as she sat down in her mother's big chair.

"It wasn't dreadful, Jo, only so sad! I saw in a minute that it was sicker, but Lottchen said her mother had gone for a doctor, so I took Baby and let Lotty rest. It seemed asleep, but all of a sudden it gave a little cry and trembled, and then lay still. I tried to warm its feet, and Lotty gave it some milk, but it didn't stir, and I knew it was dead."

"Don't cry, dear! What did you do?"

"I just sat and held it softly till Mrs. Hummel came with the doctor. He said it was dead, and looked at Heinrich and Minna, who have sore throats. 'Scarlet fever, ma'am. Ought to have called me before,' he said crossly. Mrs. Hummel told him she was poor, and had tried to cure the baby herself, and she could only ask him to help the others as charity. He smiled then, and was kinder, but it was very sad. He told me to go home and take belladonna right away, or I'd have the fever."

"No, you won't!" cried Jo, hugging her close, with a frightened look. "Oh, Beth, if you should be sick I never could forgive myself."

"I guess I shan't have it badly. I looked in Mother's book, and saw that it begins with headache, sore throat, and strange feelings like mine, so I did take some belladonna, and I feel better," said Beth, laying her cold hands on her hot forehead and trying to look well.

"If Mother was only at home!" exclaimed Jo, seizing the book, and feeling that Washington was an immense way off. She read a page, looked at Beth, felt her head, peeped into her throat, and then said gravely, "You've been over the baby every day for more than a week. So I'm afraid you are going to have it, Beth. I'll call Hannah, she knows all about sickness."

"Don't let Amy come. She never had it, and I should hate to give it to her. Can you and Meg have it over again?" asked Beth, anxiously.

"I guess not. I don't care if I do—it serves me right, selfish pig, to let you go and stay writing rubbish," muttered Jo, as she went to consult Hannah.

The good soul was wide awake in a minute and took the lead at once, assuring Jo that there was no need to worry. Everyone had scarlet fever, and if rightly treated, nobody died.

"Now I'll tell you what we'll do," said Hannah, when she had examined and questioned Beth. "We will have Dr. Bangs take a look at you, dear, and see that we start right. Then we'll send Amy off to Aunt March's for a spell, to keep her out of harm's way, and one of you girls can stay home from work and amuse Beth for a day or two. Which will you have, Beth?"

"Jo, please." And Beth leaned her head against her sister with a contented look, which settled that point.

"I'll go and tell Amy," said Meg, feeling a little hurt, yet relieved on the whole, for she did not like nursing, and Jo did.

Amy declared that she had rather have the fever than go to Aunt March. Meg reasoned, pleaded, and commanded—all in vain. Laurie walked into the parlor to find Amy sobbing, with her head in the sofa cushions. She told her story, expecting to be consoled, but Laurie knit his brows in deep thought. Presently he sat down beside her and said in his most wheedlesome tone, "Now be a sensible little woman, and do as they say. No, don't cry, but hear what a jolly plan I've got. You go to Aunt March's, and I'll come and take you out every day, driving or walking, and we'll have capital times. Won't that be better than moping here?"

"I dare say I shall be sick, for I've been with Beth all the time."

"That's the very reason you ought to go away at once, so that you may escape it or have it more lightly. I advise you to be off as soon as you can, for scarlet fever is no joke, miss."

"But it's dull at Aunt March's, and she is so cross," said Amy, looking frightened.

"It won't be dull with me popping in every day to tell you how Beth is and taking you out gallivanting. The old lady likes me, and I'll be as sweet as possible to her, so she won't peck at us, whatever we do."

"Will you bring me back the minute Beth is well?"

"The identical minute."

"And go to the theater, truly?"

"A dozen theaters, if we may."

"Well—I guess—I will," said Amy slowly.

"Good girl! Call Meg, and tell her you'll give in," said Laurie, with an approving pat, which annoyed Amy more than the "giving in."

Meg and Jo came running down to behold the miracle which had been wrought, and Amy, feeling precious and self-sacrificing, promised to go if the doctor said Beth was going to be ill.

"How is Beth?" asked Laurie, for she was his special pet, and he felt more anxious about her than he liked to show.

"She is lying down on Mother's bed, and feels better. The baby's death troubled her, but I dare say she has only caught cold. Hannah says she thinks so, but she looks worried, and that makes me fidgety," answered Meg.

"What a trying world it is!" said Jo, rumpling up her hair in a fretful sort of way. "No sooner do we get out of one trouble than down comes another. There doesn't seem to be anything to hold on to when Mother's gone, so I'm all at sea."

"Well, don't make a porcupine of yourself, it isn't becoming. Settle your wig, Jo, and tell me if I shall send a telegraph to your mother, or do anything!" asked Laurie, who still regretted the loss of his friend's one beauty.

"That is what troubles me," said Meg. "I think we ought to tell her, but Hannah says we mustn't. Beth won't be sick long, and Hannah knows just what to do, and Mother said we were to mind her, so I suppose we must, but it doesn't seem quite right to me."

"Hum, well, I can't say. Suppose you ask Grandfather after the doctor has come."

"We will. Jo, go and get Dr. Bangs at once," commanded Meg. "We can't decide anything till he has come."

"Stay where you are, Jo. I'm errand boy to this establishment," said Laurie, taking up his cap. "I've done my lessons for the day."

"Do you study in vacation time?" asked Jo.

"I follow the good example my neighbors set me" was Laurie's answer, as he swung himself out of the room.

"I have great hopes for my boy," observed Jo, watching him fly over the fence with an approving smile.

"He does very well—for a boy" was Meg's somewhat ungracious answer, for the subject did not interest her.

Dr. Bangs came, said Beth had symptoms of the fever, but thought she would have it lightly, though he looked sober over the Hummel story. Amy was ordered off at once, with Jo and Laurie as escort.

Aunt March received them with her usual hospitality.

"What do you want now?" she asked, looking sharply over her spectacles, while the parrot, sitting on the back of her chair, called out, "Go away. No boys allowed here."

Jo told her story.

"No more than I expected, if you are allowed to go poking about among poor folks. Amy can stay and make herself useful if she isn't sick, which I've no doubt she will be—looks like it now. Don't cry, child, it bothers me to hear people sniff."

Amy *was* on the point of crying, but Laurie slyly pulled the parrot's tail, which caused Polly to utter an astonished croak and call out, "Bless my boots!" in such a funny way that she laughed instead.

"What do you hear from your mother?" asked the old lady gruffly.

"Father is much better," replied Jo, trying to keep sober.

"Oh, is he? Well, that won't last long, I fancy. He never had any stamina," was the cheerful reply.

"Ha, ha! Never say die, take a pinch of snuff, goodbye, goodbye!" squalled Polly, dancing on her perch and clawing at the old lady's cap as Laurie tweaked him in the rear.

"Hold your tongue, you disrespectful old bird! And, Jo, you'd better go at once. It isn't proper to be gadding about so late with a rattle-pated boy like . . ."

"Hold your tongue, you disrespectful old bird!" cried Polly, tumbling off the chair with a bounce, and running to peck the "rattlepated" boy who was shaking with laughter.

"I don't think I *can* bear it, but I'll try," thought Amy, as she was left alone with Aunt March.

"Get along, you fright!" screamed Polly, and at that rude speech Amy could not restrain a sniff.

18

DARK DAYS

BETH DID HAVE SCARLET FEVER, and was much sicker than anyone but Hannah and the doctor suspected. The girls knew nothing about illness. Meg stayed at home, lest she should infect the Kings, and kept house, feeling a little guilty when she wrote letters in which no mention was made of Beth's illness. She could not think it right to deceive her mother, but she had been told to mind Hannah, and Hannah wouldn't hear of "Mrs. March bein' told, and worried just for sech a trifle."

Jo devoted herself to Beth day and night. But there came a time when during the fever fits she began to talk in a hoarse, broken voice, to play on the coverlet as if on her beloved little piano, and try to sing with a throat so swollen that there was no music left. Soon she did not know the familiar faces round her, but addressed them by wrong names, and called imploringly for her mother. Then Jo grew frightened, Meg begged to be allowed to write the truth, and even Hannah said she "would think of it, though there was no danger *yet.*" A letter from Washington added to their trouble, for Mr. March had had a relapse, and could not think of coming home for a long while.

How dark the days seemed now while the shadow of death hovered over the once happy home! Then it was that Margaret, sitting alone

Jo devoted herself to Beth day and night.

with tears dropping often on her work, felt how rich she had been in things more precious than any luxuries money could buy—in love, protection, peace, and health, the real blessings of life. Then it was that Jo, living in the darkened room with that suffering little sister, learned to see the beauty and the sweetness of Beth's nature, to feel how deep and tender a place she filled in all hearts, and to value Beth's unselfish ambition to live for others and to make home happy with simple virtues better than talent, wealth, or beauty. And Amy, in her exile, longed eagerly to be at home, feeling now that no service would be hard or irksome, and remembering how many neglected tasks Beth's willing hands had done for her.

Laurie haunted the house like a restless ghost, and Mr. Laurence locked the grand piano. Everyone missed Beth. The milkman, baker, grocer, and butcher inquired how she did, poor Mrs. Hummel came to beg forgiveness and to tell that Minna had died, the neighbors sent all sorts of comforts and good wishes, and even those who knew her best were surprised to find how many friends shy little Beth had made.

Meanwhile she lay on her bed with old Joanna at her side. She longed for her cats, but would not have them there lest they should get sick. She sent loving messages to Amy, bade them tell her mother that she would write soon, and often begged for pencil and paper to try to say a word, that Father might not think she had neglected him. But soon even these intervals of consciousness ended, and she lay hour after hour, tossing to and fro, with incoherent words on her lips, or sank into a heavy sleep which brought her no refreshment. Dr. Bangs came twice a day, Hannah sat up at night, Meg kept a telegram in her desk all ready to send off at any minute, and Jo never stirred from Beth's side.

The first of December was a wintry day indeed to them, for a bitter wind blew, snow fell fast, and the year seemed getting ready for its death. When Dr. Bangs came that morning, he looked long at Beth, held the hot hand in both his own a minute, and laid it gently down, saying, in a low tone to Hannah, "If Mrs. March *can* leave her husband, she'd better be sent for."

Hannah nodded without speaking, for her lips twitched nervously. Meg dropped down into a chair as the strength seemed to go out of her limbs at the sound of those words, and Jo, after standing with a pale face for a minute, ran to the parlor, snatched up the telegram, and, throwing on her things, rushed out into the storm. She was soon back, and Laurie came in with a letter saying that Mr. March was mending again. Jo read it thankfully, but her face was so full of misery that Laurie asked quickly, "What is it? Is Beth worse?"

"I've sent for Mother," said Jo, tugging at her rubber boots with a tragic expression.

"Good for you, Jo! Did you do it on your own?" asked Laurie, as he seated her in the hall chair and took off the rebellious boots, seeing how her hands shook.

"No, the doctor told us to."

"Oh, Jo, it's not so bad as that?" cried Laurie, with a startled face.

"Yes, it is. She doesn't know us, she doesn't even talk about the flocks of green doves, as she calls the vine leaves on the wall. She doesn't look like my Beth, and there's nobody to help us bear it. Mother and Father are both gone, and God seems so far away I can't find Him."

As the tears streamed fast down poor Jo's cheeks, she stretched out her hand in a helpless sort of way, as if groping in the dark, and Laurie took it in his, whispering as well as he could with a lump in his throat, "I'm here. Hold on to me, Jo, dear!"

She could not speak, but she did "hold on," and the warm grasp of the friendly human hand comforted her sore heart, and seemed to lead her nearer to the Divine arms which alone could uphold her in her trouble. Laurie longed to say something tender and comfortable, but no fitting words came to him, so he stood silently, gently stroking her bent head as her mother used to do. It was the best thing he could have done, far more soothing than the most eloquent words, for Jo felt the unspoken sympathy. Soon she dried the tears which had relieved her, and looked up with a grateful face.

"Thank you, Teddy, I'm better now. I don't feel so forlorn, and will try to bear it if it comes."

"Keep hoping for the best, that will help you, Jo. Soon your mother will be here, and then everything will be right."

"I'm so glad Father is better. Now she won't feel so bad about leaving him. Oh, me! It does seem as if all the troubles came in a heap, and I got the heaviest part on my shoulders," sighed Jo, spreading her wet handkerchief over her knees to dry.

"Doesn't Meg pull fair?" asked Laurie, looking indignant.

"Oh, yes, she tries to, but she can't love Bethy as I do, and she won't miss her as I shall. Beth is my conscience, and I can't give her up. I can't!"

Down went Jo's face into the wet handkerchief, and she cried despairingly, for she had kept up bravely till now and never shed a tear. Laurie could not speak till he had subdued the choky feeling in his throat and steadied his lips. Presently, as Jo's sobs quieted, he said hopefully, "I don't think she will die. She's so good, and we all love her so much, I don't believe God will take her away yet."

"The good and dear people always do die," groaned Jo, but she stopped crying, for her friend's words cheered her up in spite of her own doubts and fears. "You are a good doctor, Teddy, and *such* a comforting friend. How can I ever pay you?"

"I'll send in my bill, by-and-by, and now I'll give you some good medicine," said Laurie, beaming at her.

"What is it?" cried Jo.

"I telegraphed to your mother yesterday, and Brooke answered she'd come at once. She'll be here tonight, and everything will be all right. Aren't you glad I did it?"

Laurie spoke fast, and turned red and excited all in a minute, for he had kept his plot a secret for fear of disappointing the girls or harming

Beth. Jo turned white, flew out of her chair, and the moment he stopped speaking she electrified him by throwing her arms around his neck, and crying out, with a joyful cry, "Oh, Laurie! Oh, Mother! I'm so glad!" She laughed hysterically, and trembled and clung to her friend.

Laurie, though decidedly amazed, behaved with great presence of mind. He patted her back soothingly, and finding that she was recovering, followed it up by a bashful kiss or two, which brought Jo round at once. Holding on to the banisters, she gently pushed him away, saying breathlessly, "Oh, don't! I didn't mean to, it was dreadful of me, but you were such a dear to go and do it in spite of Hannah that I couldn't help flying at you."

"I don't mind," laughed Laurie, as he settled his tie. "Why, you see I got fidgety, and so did Grandpa. We thought Hannah was overdoing the authority business, and your mother ought to know. She'd never forgive us if Beth—well, if anything happened, you know. So I got Grandpa to say it was high time we did something, and off I pelted to the office yesterday. Your mother will come, I know, and the late train is in at 2:00 A.M. I shall go for her, and you've only got to bottle up your rapture, and keep Beth quiet till that blessed lady gets here."

"Laurie, you're an angel! How shall I ever thank you?"

"Fly at me again. I rather like it," said Laurie, looking mischievous.

"No, thank you. Don't tease, but go home and rest, for you'll be up half the night. Bless you, Teddy, bless you!"

"That's the interferingest chap I ever see, but I forgive him and do hope Mrs. March is coming on right away," said Hannah, with an air of relief when Jo told the good news.

Meg had a quiet rapture, and then brooded over the letter, while Jo set the sickroom in order, and Hannah "whipped up a couple of pies in case of company unexpected." A breath of fresh air seemed to blow through the house, and something better than sunshine brightened the quiet rooms. Everything appeared to feel the hopeful change.

Beth's bird began to chirp again, and a rose bud was discovered on Amy's bush in the window. The fires seemed to burn with unusual cheeriness, and every time the girls met, their pale faces broke into smiles as they hugged one another, whispering encouragingly, "Mother's coming! Mother's coming!"

Every one rejoiced but Beth. She lay in that heavy stupor, unconscious of hope and joy, doubt and danger. It was a piteous sight—the once rosy face so changed and vacant, the once busy hands so weak and wasted, the once smiling lips silent, and the once pretty, well-kept hair scattered rough and tangled on the pillow. All day she lay so, only rousing now and then to mutter, "Water!" with lips so parched they could hardly shape the word. All day Jo and Meg hovered over her, watching, waiting, hoping, and trusting in God and Mother. And all day the snow fell, the bitter wind raged, and the hours dragged slowly by. But night came at last, and every time the clock struck, the sisters, still sitting on either side of the bed, looked at each other with brightening eyes, for each hour brought help nearer. The doctor had been in to say that some change, for better or worse, would probably take place about midnight, when he would return.

Hannah, quite worn out, lay down on the sofa at the bed's foot and fell fast asleep. Mr. Laurence marched to and fro in the parlor. Laurie lay on the rug, pretending to rest, but staring into the fire with the thoughtful look which made his black eyes beautifully soft and clear.

The girls never forgot that night, for no sleep came to them as they kept their watch, with that dreadful sense of powerlessness which comes to us in hours like those.

"If God spares Beth, I never will complain again," whispered Meg earnestly.

"If God spares Beth, I'll try to love and serve Him all my life," answered Jo, with equal fervor.

"I wish I had no heart, it aches so," sighed Meg, after a pause.

"If life is often as hard as this, I don't see how we ever shall get through it," added her sister, despondently.

Here the clock struck twelve, and both forgot themselves in watching Beth, for they fancied a change passed over her wan face. The house was still as death, and nothing but the wailing of the wind broke the deep hush. Weary Hannah slept on, and no one but the sisters saw the pale shadow which seemed to fall upon the little bed. An hour went by, and nothing happened except Laurie's quiet departure for the station. Another hour—still no one came, and anxious fears of delay in the storm, or accidents by the way, or, worst of all, a great grief at Washington, haunted the poor girls.

It was past two when Jo, who stood at the window thinking how dreary the world looked in its winding sheet of snow, heard a movement by the bed, and, turning quickly, saw Meg kneeling before their mother's easy chair with her face hidden. A dreadful fear passed coldly over Jo, and she thought, "Beth is dead, and Meg is afraid to tell me."

To her excited eyes a great change seemed to have taken place. The fever flush and the look of pain were gone, and the beloved little face looked so pale and peaceful in its utter repose that Jo felt no desire to weep. Leaning low over this dearest sister, she kissed the damp forehead with her heart on her lips, and softly whispered, "Goodbye, my Beth, goodbye!"

As if waked by the stir, Hannah started out of her sleep, hurried to the bed, looked at Beth, felt her hands, listened at her lips, and then, throwing her apron over her head, began to rock to and fro, exclaiming, under her breath, "The fever's turned, she's sleepin' nat'ral, her skin's damp, and she breathes easy. Praise be given! Oh, my goodness me!"

Before the girls could believe the happy truth, the doctor came to confirm it. He was a homely man, but they thought his face quite heavenly when he smiled and said, with a fatherly look at them, "Yes, my dears, I think the little girl will pull through this time. Keep the house quiet, let her sleep, and when she wakes, give her . . ."

What they were to give, neither heard, for both crept into the dark hall, and, sitting on the stairs, held each other close, rejoicing with hearts too full for words. When they went back to be kissed by faithful Hannah, they found Beth lying, as she used to do, with her cheek pillowed on her hand, the dreadful pallor gone, and breathing quietly, as if just fallen asleep.

"If Mother would only come now!" said Jo, as the winter night began to wane.

"See," said Meg, coming up with a white, half-opened rose, "I thought this would not be ready to lay in Beth's hand tomorrow if she . . . went away from us. But it has blossomed in the night, and now I mean to put it in my vase here, so that when the darling wakes, the first thing she sees will be the little rose, and Mother's face."

Never had the sun risen so beautifully, and never had the world seemed so lovely as it did to the heavy eyes of Meg and Jo, as they looked out in the early morning, when their long, sad vigil was done.

"It looks like a fairy world," said Meg, smiling to herself, as she stood behind the curtain, watching the dazzling sight.

"Listen!" cried Jo, starting to her feet.

Yes, there was a sound of bells at the door below, a cry from Hannah, and then Laurie's voice saying in a joyful whisper, "Girls, she's come! She's come."

19
AMY'S WILL

WHILE THESE THINGS were happening at home, Amy was having hard times at Aunt March's. For the first time in her life, she realized how much she was loved at home. Aunt March meant to be kind, for the well-behaved girl pleased her very much, and Aunt March had a soft place in her heart for her nephew's children, though she didn't think it proper to confess it. She really did her best to make Amy happy, but what mistakes she made! Some old people keep young at heart in spite of wrinkles and gray hairs, but Aunt March did not have this gift. Finding Amy more docile and amiable than her sister, the old lady felt it her duty to try and counteract, as far as possible, the bad effects of home freedom. So she took her in hand, and taught her as she herself had been taught sixty years ago—a process which dismayed Amy and made her feel like a fly in the web of a strict spider.

She had to wash the cups every morning, and polish up the old-fashioned spoons, the fat silver teapot, and the glasses till they shone. Then she must dust the room, and what a trying job that was! Not a speck escaped Aunt March's eye, and all the furniture had claw legs and much carving, which was never dusted to suit. Then Polly must be fed, the lap dog combed, and a dozen trips upstairs and down to get things or deliver orders, for the old lady was lame and seldom left her big chair. After these tiresome labors, she must do her lessons. Then she was allowed one hour for exercise or play, and didn't she enjoy it! Laurie came every day, and wheedled Aunt March till Amy was allowed to go out with him, when they had capital times. After dinner, she had to read aloud, and sit still while the old lady slept, which she usually did for an hour, as she dropped off over the first page. Then patchwork or towels appeared, and Amy sewed with outward meekness and inward rebellion till dusk, when she was allowed to amuse herself as she liked till teatime. The evenings were the worst of all, for Aunt March fell to telling long stories about her youth, which were so dull that Amy was always ready to go to bed, intending to cry over her hard fate, but usually going to sleep before she had squeezed out more than a tear or two.

If it had not been for Laurie, and old Esther, the maid, she felt that she never could have gotten through that dreadful time. The parrot alone was enough to drive her distracted, for he was as mischievous as possible. He pulled her hair whenever she came near him, upset his bread and milk to plague her when she had newly cleaned his cage, made Mop bark by pecking at him while Madam dozed, called her names before company, and behaved in all respects like a reprehensible old bird. She could not endure the dog—a fat, cross beast who snarled and yelped at her when she combed him, and who lay on his back with all his legs in the air and a most idiotic expression when he wanted something to eat, which was about a dozen times a day. The cook was bad-tempered, the old coachman deaf, and Esther the only one who ever took any notice of her.

Esther was a Frenchwoman, who had lived with "Madame," as she called her mistress, for many years. Her real name was Estelle, but Aunt March ordered her to change it and she obeyed, on condition that she was never asked to change her religion. She took a fancy to Mademoiselle, and amused her with odd stories of her life in France. She also allowed her to roam about the great house, and examine the curious and pretty things stored away in the big wardrobes and the ancient chests, for Aunt March hoarded like a magpie. Amy's chief delight was an Indian cabinet, full of peculiar drawers, little pigeon-holes, and secret places, in which were kept all sorts of ornaments, some precious, some merely curious, all more or less antique. To examine and arrange these things gave Amy great satisfaction, especially the jewel cases. There were the pearls her father gave her on her wedding day, her lover's diamonds, lockets with portraits of dead friends and weeping willows made of hair inside, the baby bracelets her one little daughter had worn, Uncle March's big watch, and in a box all by itself lay Aunt March's wedding ring, too small now for her fat finger, but put carefully away like the most precious jewel of them all.

"Which would Mademoiselle choose?" asked Esther, who always sat near to watch over and lock up the valuables.

"I like the diamonds best, but there is no necklace among them, and I'm fond of necklaces, they are so becoming. I should choose this if I might," replied Amy, looking with great admiration at a string of gold and ebony beads from which hung a heavy cross.

"I, too, covet that, but not as a necklace. Ah, no! To me it is a rosary for prayer, and as such I should use it like a good Catholic," said Esther, eying the handsome thing wistfully.

"As you use the string of good-smelling wooden beads hanging over your mirror?" asked Amy. "You seem to take a great deal of comfort from your prayers, Esther. I wish I could."

"If Mademoiselle was a Catholic, she would find true comfort. But as that is not to be, it would be well if you went apart each day to pray, as did the good mistress whom I served before Madame. She had a little chapel and in it found solace for much trouble."

"Would it be right for me to do so, too?" asked Amy, who in her loneliness felt the need of help of some sort, and found that she was apt to forget her little book, now that Beth was not there to remind her of it.

"It would be excellent and charming, and I shall gladly arrange the little dressing room for you if you like it. Say nothing to Madame, but when she sleeps go and sit alone a while to think good thoughts, and pray the dear God to preserve your sister." Esther was truly pious and sincere in her advice, for she had an affectionate heart, and felt much for the sisters in their anxiety.

"I wish I knew where all these pretty things would go when Aunt March dies," Amy said, as she slowly replaced the shining rosary and shut the jewel cases one by one.

"To you and your sisters. I know it, Madame confides in me. I witnessed her will, and it is to be so," whispered Esther, smiling.

"How nice! But I wish she'd let us have them now. Pro-cras-ti-nation is not agreeable," observed Amy, taking a last look at the diamonds.

"It is too soon yet for the young ladies to wear these things. The first one who is engaged will have the pearls—Madame has said it—and I have a fancy that the little turquoise ring will be given to you soon, for Madame approves your good behavior and charming manners."

"Do you think so? Oh, I'll be a lamb, if I can only have that lovely ring! It's ever so much prettier than Kitty Bryant's. I do like Aunt March, after all." And Amy tried on the blue ring with a delighted face and a firm resolve to earn it.

From that day she was a model of obedience. Esther fitted up the closet with a little table, placed a footstool before it, and over it a picture taken from one of the closed-off rooms. She thought it was of no great value, but it was a copy of one of the famous pictures of the world, and Amy's beauty-loving eyes were never tired of looking up at the sweet face of the divine mother. On the table she laid her little Testament and hymn-book, kept a vase always full of the best flowers Laurie brought her, and came every day to "sit alone, thinking good thoughts, and praying the dear God to preserve her sister." Esther had given her a rosary of black beads with a silver cross, but Amy hung it up and did not use it, feeling doubtful as to its fitness for Protestant prayers.

Being left alone outside the safe home nest, she instinctively turned to the strong and tender Friend, whose fatherly love most closely surrounds his little children. But Amy was a young pilgrim, and just now her burden seemed heavy. She tried to forget herself, to keep cheerful, and to be satisfied with doing right, though no one saw or praised her for it. In her first effort at being very, very good, she decided to make her will, as Aunt March had done, so that if she *did* fall ill and die, her possessions might be justly and generously divided. It cost her a pang even to think of giving up the little treasures which in her eyes were as precious as the old lady's jewels.

One day she wrote out the important document as well as she could, with some help from Esther. As it was rainy, she went upstairs to amuse herself in one of the large chambers, and took Polly with her for company. In this room there was a wardrobe full of old fashioned costumes, and it was her favorite amusement to array herself in the faded brocades, and parade up and down before the long mirror. She did not hear Laurie's ring nor see his face peeping in at her as she gravely promenaded to and fro, flirting her fan and tossing her head. It was a comical sight to see her mince along in high-heeled shoes, with Polly sidling and bridling just behind her, imitating her as well as he could, and occasionally stopping to laugh or exclaim, "Ain't we fine? Get along, you fright! Hold your tongue! Kiss me, dear! Ha, ha!"

Laurie was graciously received. "Sit down and rest while I put these things away, then I want to consult you about a very serious matter," said Amy. "That bird is the trial of my life," she continued, removing the pink turban from her head, while Laurie seated himself astride a chair. "Yesterday, when Aunt was asleep and I was trying to be as still as a mouse, Polly began to squall and flap about in his cage. So I went to let him out, and found a big spider there. I poked it out, and it ran under the bookcase. Polly marched straight after it, stooped down and peeped under the bookcase, saying with a cock of his eye, 'Come out and take a walk, my dear.' I couldn't help laughing, which made Poll swear, and Aunt woke up and scolded us."

"I'd wring your neck if you were mine, you old torment," cried Laurie, shaking his fist at the bird, who put his head on one side and gravely croaked, "Allyluyer! Bless your buttons, dear!"

"Now I'm ready," said Amy, shutting the wardrobe and taking a paper out of her pocket. "I want you to read that, please, and tell me if it is legal and right. I felt that I ought to do it, for life is uncertain and I don't want any ill feeling over my tomb."

Laurie bit his lips, and turning a little from the pensive speaker, read the following document, with praiseworthy gravity, considering the spelling:

MY LAST WILL AND TESTIMENT

I, Amy Curtis March, being in my sane mind, do give and bequeethe all my earthly property—viz. to wit:—namely

To my father, my best pictures, sketches, maps, and works of art, including frames. Also my $100, to do what he likes with.

To my mother, all my clothes, except the blue apron with pockets—also my likeness, and my medal, with much love.

To my dear sister Margaret, I give my turkquoise ring (if I get it), also my green box with the doves on it, also my piece of real lace for her neck, and my sketch of her as a memorial of her "little girl."

To Jo I leave my breastpin, the one mended with sealing wax, also my bronze inkstand—she lost the cover—and my most precious plaster rabbit, because I am sorry I burned up her story.

To Beth (if she lives after me) I give my dolls and the little bureau, my fan, my linen collars and my new slippers if she can wear them being thin when she gets well. And I herewith also leave her my regret that I ever made fun of old Joanna.

To my friend and neighbor Theodore Laurence I bequeethe my paper mashay portfolio, my clay model of a horse though he did say it hadn't any neck. Also in return for his great kindness in the hour of affliction any one of my artistic works he likes, Noter Dame is the best.

To our venerable benefactor Mr. Laurence I leave my Purple box with a looking glass in the cover which will be nice for his pens and remind him of the departed girl who thanks him for his favors to her family, specially Beth.

I wish my favorite playmate Kitty Bryant to have the blue silk apron and my gold-bead ring with a kiss.

To Hannah I give the bandbox she wanted and all the patch-work I leave hoping she "will remember me, when it you see."

And now having disposed of my most valuable property I hope all will be satisfied and not blame the dead. I forgive everyone, and trust we may all meet when the trump shall sound. Amen.

To this will and testament I set my hand and seal on this 20th day of Nov. Anni Domino 1861.

Amy Curtis March

Witnesses:
        ESTELLE VALNOR.
        THEODORE LAURENCE.

The last name was written in pencil, and Amy explained that he was to rewrite it in ink and seal it up for her properly.

"What put it into your head? Did anyone tell you about Beth's giving away her things?" asked Laurie soberly.

She explained and then asked anxiously, "What about Beth?"

"I'm sorry I spoke, but I'll tell you. She felt so ill one day that she told Jo she wanted to give her piano to Meg, her cats to you, and the poor old doll to Jo, who would love it for her sake. She was sorry she had so little to give, and left locks of hair to the rest of us, and her best love to Grandpa. She never thought of a will."

Laurie was signing and sealing as he spoke, and did not look up till a great tear dropped on the paper. Amy said, "Don't people put sort of postscripts to their wills, sometimes?"

"Yes, 'codicils,' they call them."

"Put one in mine then—that I wish all my curls cut off, and given round to my friends. I forgot it, but I want it done, though it will spoil my looks."

Laurie added it, smiling at Amy's last and greatest sacrifice. But when he came to go, Amy held him back to whisper with trembling lips, "Is there any danger about Beth?"

"I'm afraid there is, but we must hope for the best, so don't cry, dear." And Laurie put his arm about her with a brotherly gesture that was comforting.

When he had gone, she went to her little chapel, and sitting in the twilight, prayed for Beth, with streaming tears and an aching heart, feeling that a million turquoise rings would not console her for the loss of her gentle sister.

20
CONFIDENTIAL

WHEN BETH WOKE from that long, healing sleep, the first objects on which her eyes fell were the little rose and Mother's face. Too weak to wonder at anything, she only smiled and nestled close into the loving arms about her, feeling that the hungry longing was satisfied at last. Then she slept again.

Hannah had "dished up" an astonishing breakfast for the traveler. Meg and Jo listened to her whispered account of Father's state, Mr. Brooke's promise to stay and nurse him, the delays the storm caused on the homeward journey, and the unspeakable comfort Laurie's hopeful face had given her when she arrived, worn out with fatigue, anxiety, and cold.

What a strange yet pleasant day that was! So brilliant and merry without, for all the world seemed abroad to welcome the first snow; so quiet within, for everyone slept. Meg and Jo closed their weary eyes and lay at rest, like storm-beaten boats safe at anchor in a quiet harbor. Mrs. March would not leave Beth's side, but rested in the big chair, waking often to look at, touch, and brood over her child, like a miser over some recovered treasure.

Laurie hurried off to comfort Amy, and told his story so well that Aunt March never once said, "I told you so." It seems the good thoughts in the little chapel began to bear fruit, because Amy dried her tears quickly and restrained her impatience to see her mother, without even a thought of the turquoise ring. Even Polly seemed impressed with her, for he called her "good girl," blessed her buttons, and begged her to "come and take a walk, dear," in his most affable tone. She would gladly have gone out to enjoy the bright wintry weather, but she persuaded Laurie to rest on the sofa, while she wrote a note to her mother. She was a long time about it, and when she returned, he was stretched out with both arms under his head, sound asleep.

He was finally roused by Amy's cry of joy at the sight of her mother. There probably were a good many happy little girls in and about the city that day, but Amy was the happiest of all when she sat in her mother's lap and told her trials. They were alone together in the chapel, to which her mother did not object when its purpose was explained.

"On the contrary, I like it very much, dear," looking from the dusty rosary to the well-worn little book, and the lovely picture with its garland of evergreen. "It is an excellent plan to have some place where we can go to be quiet, when things vex or grieve us. There are a good many hard times in this life of ours, but we can always bear them if we ask help in the right way. I think my little girl is learning this."

"Yes, Mother, and when I go home I mean to have a corner in the big closet to put my books and this copy of the picture which I've tried to make. My woman's face is not good—it's too beautiful for me to draw, but the baby is done better, and I love it very much. I like to think He was a little child once, for then I don't seem so far away, and that helps me."

As Amy pointed to the smiling Christ child on his mother's knee, Mrs. March saw something on the lifted hand that made her smile. She said nothing, but Amy understood the look, and after a minute's pause, she added gravely, "Aunt gave me the ring today. She called me to her and kissed me, and put it on my finger, and said I was a credit to her, and she'd like to keep me always. She gave me this funny ring guard, as the ring is too big. I'd like to wear them, Mother, can I?"

"They are pretty, but I think you're too young for such ornaments, Amy," said Mrs. March, looking at the plump little hand, with the band of sky-blue stones on the forefinger, and the quaint guard formed of two tiny golden hands clasped together.

"I'll try not to be vain," said Amy. "I like it because it's so pretty, but I want to wear it to remind me not to be selfish." Amy looked so earnest and sincere that her mother listened respectfully to her little plan.

"I've thought a great deal lately about my 'bundle of naughties,' and being selfish is the largest one in it. So I'm going to try hard to cure it, if I can. Beth isn't selfish, and that's the reason everyone loves her and feels so bad at the thought of losing her. People wouldn't feel half so bad about me if I was sick. But I'd like to be loved and missed by a great many friends, so I'm going to try and be like Beth all I can. If I had something always with me to remind me, I think I should do better. May I try this way?"

"Yes, but I have more faith in the corner of the big closet. Wear your ring, dear, and do your best. I think you will prosper, for the sincere wish to be good is half the battle. Now I must go back to Beth. Keep up your heart, little daughter, and we will soon have you home again."

That evening, while Meg was writing to her father, Jo slipped upstairs into Beth's room, and finding her mother in her usual place, stood a minute twisting her fingers in her hair, looking worried and undecided.

"What is it, deary?" asked Mrs. March, holding out her hand.

"I want to tell you something, Mother."

"About Meg?"

"How quickly you guessed!" said Jo, settling herself on the floor at her mother's feet. "Last summer Meg left a pair of gloves over at the Laurences' and only one was returned. We forgot all about it, till Teddy told me that Mr. Brooke had it. He keeps it in his waistcoat pocket, and once it fell out, and Teddy teased him about it, and Mr. Brooke owned that he liked Meg but didn't dare say so, she was so young and he so poor. Now, isn't it a *dread*ful state of things?"

"Do you think Meg cares for him?" asked Mrs. March, with an anxious look.

"Mercy me! I don't know anything about love and such nonsense!" cried Jo, with a funny mixture of interest and contempt. "Meg eats and drinks and sleeps like a sensible creature, she looks straight in my face when I talk about that man, and only blushes a little bit when Teddy jokes about lovers. I forbid him to do it, but he doesn't mind me as he ought."

"Then you fancy that Meg is not interested in John?"

"Who?" cried Jo, staring.

"Mr. Brooke. I call him John now. We fell into the way of doing so at the hospital, and he likes it. He was so devoted to poor Father that we couldn't help getting fond of him. He told us he loved Meg, but would earn a comfortable home before he asked her to marry him. He only wanted our leave to love her and work for her, and the right to make her love him if he could. He is a truly excellent young man, but I will not consent to Meg's engaging herself so young."

"Of course not. It would be idiotic! I knew there was mischief brewing, I felt it, and now it's worse than I imagined. I just wish I could marry Meg myself, and keep her safe in the family."

This odd arrangement made Mrs. March smile, but she said gravely, "Jo, I confide in you and don't wish you to say anything to Meg yet."

"She's got such a soft heart it will melt like butter in the sun if anyone looks sentimentally at her. She'll go and fall in love, and there's an end of peace and fun, and cozy times together. I see it all! They'll go lovering around the house. Brooke will scratch up a fortune somehow, carry her off, and make a hole in the family, and it shall break my heart. Oh, dear me! Why weren't we all boys, then there wouldn't be any bother."

"Meg is only seventeen and it will be some years before John can make a home for her. Your father and I have agreed that she shall not bind herself in any way, nor be married, before twenty. If she and John love one another, they can wait, and test the love by doing so. My pretty, tenderhearted girl! I hope things will go happily with her."

"Hadn't you rather have her marry a rich man?" asked Jo, as her mother's voice faltered a little over the last words.

"Money is a good and useful thing, Jo, and I hope my girls will never feel the need of it too bitterly nor be tempted by it too much. I'm not ambitious for a splendid fortune, a fashionable position, or a great name for my girls. If rank and money come with love and virtue, I should accept them gratefully, and enjoy your good fortune. But I know by experience how much genuine happiness can be had in a plain little house, where the daily bread is earned, and some lacks give sweetness to the pleasures. I am content to see Meg begin humbly, for if I am not mistaken, she will be rich in the possession of a good man's heart, and that is better than a fortune."

"I understand, Mother, and quite agree, but I'm disappointed about Meg, for I'd planned to have her marry Teddy by-and-by and sit in the lap of luxury all her days. Wouldn't it be nice?" asked Jo, looking up with a brighter face.

"He is younger than she, you know . . ." began Mrs. March, but Jo broke in, "Only a little. He's old for his age, and tall, and can be quite grown-up. And he's rich and generous and good, and loves us all, and *I* say it's a pity my plan is spoiled."

"I'm afraid Laurie is hardly grown-up enough for Meg. Don't make plans, Jo. We can't meddle safely in such matters, and had better not get 'romantic rubbish,' as you call it, into our heads."

"Well, I won't, but I hate to see things going all crisscross and getting snarled up, when a pull here and a snip there would straighten it out. I wish wearing flatirons on our heads would keep us from growing up. But buds will be roses, and kittens, cats. More's the pity!"

"What's that about flatirons and cats?" asked Meg, as she crept into the room with the finished letter in her hand.

184

"Only one of my stupid speeches. I'm going to bed. Come, Peggy," said Jo, unfolding herself.

"Quite right, and beautifully written. Please add that I send my love to John," said Mrs. March, as she glanced over Meg's letter and gave it back.

"Do you call him John?" asked Meg, smiling, with her innocent eyes looking down into her mother's.

"Yes, he has been like a son to us, and we are very fond of him," replied Mrs. March, returning the look with a wise one.

"I'm glad of that, he is so lonely. Good night, Mother, dear. It is so inexpressibly comfortable to have you here," was Meg's answer.

The kiss her mother gave her was a tender one, and as she went away, Mrs. March said, with a mixture of satisfaction and regret, "She does not love John yet, but will soon learn to."

21

LAURIE MAKES MISCHIEF,
AND JO MAKES PEACE

THE NEXT DAY Jo's face showed that she had a secret. Laurie no sooner suspected a mystery than he set himself to find it out. He wheedled, bribed, ridiculed, threatened, and scolded; affected indifference; declared he knew, then that he didn't care; and, at last, by dint of perseverance, he was sure that it concerned Meg and Mr. Brooke. Feeling indignant that he was left out of the secret, he set his wits to work.

All of a sudden a change seemed to come over Meg, and, for a day or two, she was unlike herself. She was startled when spoken to, blushed when looked at, was very quiet, and had a timid, troubled look on her face. To her mother's inquiries she answered that she was quite well, and Jo's she silenced by begging to be let alone.

"She feels it in the air—love, I mean. She's got most of the symptoms—is twittery and cross, doesn't eat, lies awake, and mopes in corners. I caught her singing that song he gave her, and once she said 'John,' and then turned as red as a poppy. Whatever shall we do?" said Jo, looking ready for any measures, however violent.

"Let her alone, be kind and patient, and Father's coming will settle everything," replied her mother.

"Here's a note to you, Meg, all sealed up," said Jo the next day, as she distributed the contents of the little post office.

Mrs. March and Jo were deep in their own affairs, when a sound from Meg made them look up to see her staring at her note with a frightened face. "It's all a mistake—he didn't send it. Oh, Jo, how could you?" and Meg hid her face in her hands, crying as if her heart was broken.

"Me? I've done nothing! What's she talking about?" cried Jo, bewildered.

Meg's mild eyes kindled with anger as she pulled an old crumpled note from her pocket and threw it at Jo, saying, "You wrote it, and that bad boy helped you. How could you be so mean and cruel to us both?"

Jo hardly heard her, for she and her mother were reading the old note, which was written in peculiar handwriting.

My Dearest Margaret,

I can no longer restrain my passion, and must know my fate before I return. I dare not tell your parents yet, but I think they would consent if they knew that we adored one another. Mr. Laurence will help me to some good place, and then, my sweet girl, you will make me happy. I implore you to say nothing to your family yet, but to send one word of hope through Laurie to

Your devoted John

Oh, the little villain! That's the way he meant to pay me for keeping my secret. I'll give him a scolding and bring him over to beg pardon," cried Jo, burning to execute immediate justice.

But her mother held her back, saying, with a look she seldom wore, "Stop, Jo. You have played so many pranks that I am afraid you have had a hand in this."

"On my word, Mother, I haven't! I never saw that note before, as true as I live!" said Jo, so earnestly that they believed her. "If I *had* taken a part in it I'd have done it better than this, and have written a sensible note. I should think you'd have known Mr. Brooke wouldn't write such stuff as that," she added, scornfully tossing down the paper.

"It's the same writing," faltered Meg, with the new note in her hand.

"Oh, Meg, you didn't answer it?" cried Mrs. March quickly. "Tell me the whole story," she commanded, sitting down by Meg, yet keeping hold of Jo, lest she should fly off.

"I received the first letter from Laurie, who didn't look as if he knew anything about it," began Meg, without looking up. "I meant to tell you. While I was deciding what to say, I felt like the girls in books, who have such things to do. Forgive me, Mother, I'm paid for my silliness now. I never can look him in the face again."

"What did you say to him?" asked Mrs. March.

"I only said I was too young to do anything about it yet, that I didn't wish to have secrets from you, and he must speak to Father. I was grateful for his kindness, and would be his friend, but nothing more, for a long while."

Mrs. March smiled, as if well pleased, and Jo clapped her hands, exclaiming, with a laugh, "Tell on, Meg. What did he say to that?"

"He tells me that he never sent any love letter at all, and is sorry that my roguish sister, Jo, should pull such a trick. It's very kind and respectful, but think how dreadful for me!"

Meg leaned against her mother, looking the image of despair, and Jo tramped about the room, calling Laurie names. All of a sudden she stopped, caught up the two notes, and after looking at them closely, said decidedly, "I don't believe Brooke ever saw either of these letters. Teddy wrote both to get even with me with because I wouldn't tell him my secret."

"I'll comfort Meg while you go and get Laurie, Jo. I shall sift the matter to the bottom, and put a stop to such pranks at once."

Away ran Jo, and Mrs. March gently told Meg Mr. Brooke's real feelings. Meg answered, "If John doesn't know anything about this nonsense, don't tell him, and make Jo and Laurie hold their tongues. I won't be deceived and plagued and made a fool of—it's a shame!"

The instant Laurie's step was heard in the hall, Meg fled into the study, and Mrs. March received the culprit alone. Jo had not told him why he was wanted, fearing he wouldn't come, but he knew the minute he saw Mrs. March's face, and stood twirling his hat with a guilty air which convicted him at once. Jo was sent out, but chose to march up and down the hall like a sentinel, having some fear that the prisoner might bolt. The sound of voices in the parlor rose and fell for half an hour, but what happened during that interview the girls never knew.

When they were called in, Laurie was standing by their mother with such a penitent face that Jo forgave him on the spot. Meg received his humble apology, and was much comforted when he said, "I'll never tell Brooke to my dying day—wild horses shan't drag it out of me. If you'll forgive me, Meg, I'll do anything to show how out-and-out sorry I am."

And Laurie folded his hands together with such an imploring gesture, as he spoke in his irresistibly persuasive tone, that it was impossible to frown upon him in spite of his scandalous behavior. Meg pardoned him, and Mrs. March's grave face relaxed, in spite of her efforts to keep sober, when she heard him declare that he would atone for his sins by all sorts of penances, and abase himself like a worm before the injured damsel.

Jo stood aloof, meanwhile, trying to harden her heart against him, and succeeded only in twisting her face. Laurie looked at her once or twice, but as she showed no sign of relenting, he felt injured, and turned his back on her till the others were done with him, when he made her a low bow and walked off without a word.

As soon as he had gone, she wished she had acted forgiving, and when Meg and her mother went upstairs, she felt lonely and longed for Teddy. After resisting for some time, she yielded to the impulse, and armed with a book to return, went over to the big house.

"Is Mr. Laurence in?" asked Jo, of a housemaid who was coming downstairs.

"Yes, miss, but I don't believe he's seeable just yet. He's had a scene with Mr. Laurie, who is in one of his tantrums about something, which vexes the old gentleman, so I don't dare go near him."

"Where is Laurie?"

"Shut up in his room, and he won't answer, though I've been knocking. I don't know what's to become of the dinner, for it's ready, and there's no one to eat it."

"I'll go and see what the matter is. I'm not afraid of either of them." Up went Jo, and knocked smartly on the door of Laurie's little study.

"Stop that, or I'll open the door and make you!" called out the young gentleman in a threatening tone.

Jo immediately knocked again. The door flew open, and in she bounced before Laurie could recover from his surprise. Seeing that he *was* out of temper, Jo, who knew how to manage him, assumed a contrite expression, and going down upon her knees, said meekly, "Please forgive me for being so cross. I came to make it up, and can't go away till I have."

"It's all right. Get up, and don't be a goose, Jo," he replied.

"Thank you, I will. Could I ask what's the matter? You don't look exactly easy in your mind."

"Grandfather shook me. If it had been anyone else I'd have . . ." and the injured youth finished his sentence by an energetic gesture of the right arm.

"I don't think anyone would care to try it, if you looked as much like a thundercloud as you do now. Why were you treated so?"

"Just because I wouldn't say what your mother wanted me for. I'd promised not to. No, he *would* have the truth, the whole truth, and nothing but the truth. I'd have told my part of the scrape, if I could without bringing Meg in. As I couldn't, I held my tongue, and bore the scolding till the old gentleman collared me. Then I got angry and bolted, for fear I should forget myself."

"It wasn't nice, but he's sorry, I know, so go down and make up. I'll help you."

"Hanged if I do! He ought to trust me, and not act as if I was a baby. It's no use, Jo. He's got to learn that I'm able to take care of myself, and don't need anyone's apron string to hold on by."

"What pepper pots you are!" sighed Jo. "How do you mean to settle this affair?"

"Well, he ought to beg pardon, and believe me when I say I can't tell him what the fuss's about. I won't go down till he does."

"Now, Teddy, be sensible. Let it pass, and I'll explain what I can. You can't stay here, so what's the use of being melodramatic?"

"I don't intend to stay here long, anyway. I'll slip off and take a journey somewhere, and when Grandpa misses me he'll come round fast enough."

"I dare say, but you ought not to go and worry him."

"Don't preach. I'll go to Washington and see Brooke."

"What fun you'd have! I wish I could run off, too," said Jo, forgetting her purpose in lively visions of life at the capital.

"Come on, then! Why not? You go and surprise your father, and I'll stir up old Brooke. It would be a glorious joke. Let's do it, Jo. We'll leave a letter saying we are all right, and trot off at once. I've got money enough."

For a moment Jo looked as if she would agree, for wild as the plan was, it just suited her. She longed for change, and thoughts of her father blended temptingly with the novel charms of liberty and fun. Her eyes kindled as they turned wistfully toward the window, but they fell on the old house opposite, and she shook her head with sorrowful decision.

"If I was a boy, we'd run away together and have a capital time. But as I'm a miserable girl, I must be proper and stay at home. Don't tempt me, Teddy, it's a crazy plan."

"I know Meg would wet-blanket such a proposal, but I thought you had more spirit," began Laurie cleverly.

"Bad boy, be quiet! Sit down and think of your own sins, don't go making me add to mine. If I get your grandpa to apologize for the shaking, will you give up running away?" asked Jo seriously.

"Yes, but you won't do it," answered Laurie, who wished to make up, but felt that his outraged dignity must be appeased first.

"If I can manage the young one I can the old one," muttered Jo as she walked away, leaving Laurie bent over a railroad map with his head propped up on both hands.

"Come in!" And Mr. Laurence's gruff voice sounded gruffer than ever, as Jo tapped at his door.

"It's only me, sir, come to return a book," she said blandly, as she entered.

"Want any more?" asked the old gentleman, looking grim and vexed, but trying not to show it.

Jo skipped up the library ladder and sat on the top step, as if searching for a book. But she was really wondering how best to introduce the dangerous object of her visit. Mr. Laurence seemed to suspect that something was brewing in her mind, for after taking several brisk turns about the room, he faced round on her.

"What has that boy been about? Don't try to shield him. I know he has been in mischief by the way he acted when he came home. I can't get a word from him, and when I threatened to shake the truth out of him he bolted upstairs and locked himself into his room."

"He did do wrong, but we forgave him, and all promised not to say a word to anyone," began Jo reluctantly.

"That won't do. He shall not shelter himself behind a promise from you softhearted girls. If he's done anything amiss, he shall confess, beg pardon, and be punished. Out with it, Jo, I won't be kept in the dark."

Mr. Laurence looked so alarming and spoke so sharply that Jo would have gladly run away if she could, but she was perched aloft on the steps, and he stood at the foot, a lion in the path, so she had to stay and brave it out.

"Indeed, sir, I cannot tell. Mother forbade it. Laurie has confessed, asked pardon, and been punished quite enough. We don't keep silence to shield him, but someone else, and it will make more trouble if you interfere. Please don't. It was partly my fault."

"Come down and give me your word that this harum-scarum boy of mine hasn't done anything ungrateful or impertinent. If he has, after all your kindness to him, I'll thrash him with my own hands." Jo knew the old gentleman would never lift a finger against his grandson, whatever he might say to the contrary. She obediently descended.

"If the boy held his tongue because he promised, and not from obstinacy, I'll forgive him. He's a stubborn fellow and hard to manage," said Mr. Laurence, rubbing up his hair till it looked as if he had been out in a gale, and smoothing the frown from his brow with an air of relief.

"So am I, but a kind word will govern me when all the king's horses and all the king's men couldn't," said Jo.

"You think I'm not kind to him, hey?" was the sharp answer.

"Oh, dear, no, sir. You are too kind sometimes, and then just a trifle hasty when he tries your patience. Don't you think you are?"

Jo determined to have it out now, and tried to look placid, though she quaked a little after her bold speech. To her great relief and surprise, the old gentleman only threw his spectacles onto the table with a rattle and exclaimed frankly, "You're right, girl, I am! I love the boy, but he tries my patience past bearing, and I don't know how it will end, if we go on so."

"I'll tell you, he'll run away."

Mr. Laurence's ruddy face changed suddenly, and he sat down, with a troubled glance at the picture of a handsome man, which hung over his table. It was Laurie's father, who *had* run away in his youth, and married against the old man's will. Jo fancied he remembered and regretted the past, and she wished she had held her tongue.

"He only threatens it sometimes, when he gets tired of studying," said Jo. "I often think I should like to go also, so if you ever miss us, you may advertise for two boys and look among the ships bound for India."

She laughed as she spoke, and Mr. Laurence looked relieved, evidently taking the whole as a joke.

"You hussy, how dare you talk in that way? Where's your respect for me, and your proper bringing up? Bless the boys and girls! What torments they are, yet we can't do without them. Go and bring that boy down to his dinner. Tell him it's all right, and advise him not to put on tragedy airs with his grandfather. I won't bear it."

"He won't come, sir. He feels badly because you didn't believe him when he said he couldn't tell. I think the shaking hurt his feelings very much."

Jo tried to look pathetic but must have failed, for Mr. Laurence began to laugh, and she knew the day was won.

"I'm sorry for that, and ought to thank him for not shaking me, I suppose. What the dickens does the fellow expect?"

"If I were you, I'd write him an apology, sir. Try it. He likes fun, and this way is better than talking. I'll carry it up, and teach him his duty."

Mr. Laurence gave her a sharp look, and put on his spectacles, saying slowly, "You're a sly one, but I don't mind being managed by you and Beth. Here, give me a bit of paper, and let us have done with this nonsense."

The note was written in the terms which one gentleman would use to another. Jo dropped a kiss on the top of Mr. Laurence's bald head, and ran up to slip the apology under Laurie's locked door, advising him through the keyhole to be submissive, proper, and a few other agreeable impossibilities. She left the note to do its work, and was going quietly away when the young gentleman slid down the banister, and waited for her at the bottom, saying, with his most virtuous expression, "What a good fellow you are, Jo! For a while, even you had cast me off, and I felt just ready to go to the deuce."

"Don't talk that way. Turn over a new leaf and begin again, Teddy."

"I keep turning over new leaves, and spoiling them, as I used to spoil my copybooks. I make so many beginnings there never will be an end," he said dolefully.

"You'll feel better after dinner," and Jo whisked out the front door.

Laurie went to partake of humble-pie with his grandfather, who was saintly in temper all the rest of the day.

Everyone thought the matter ended, but the mischief was done, for though others forgot it Meg remembered. She never mentioned a certain person, but she thought of him a good deal, dreamed dreams more than ever, and once Jo, rummaging her sister's desk for stamps, found a bit of paper scribbled over with the words, "Mrs. John Brooke." Jo cast it into the fire, feeling that Laurie's prank had hastened the evil day for her.

22

PLEASANT MEADOWS

LIKE SUNSHINE AFTER A STORM were the peaceful weeks that followed. Beth was soon able to lie on the study sofa all day, amusing herself with her well-beloved cats at first, and in time with dolls' sewing. Her legs were so stiff and feeble that Jo carried her about the house in her strong arms.

As Christmas approached, the usual mysteries began to haunt the house. In honor of this unusual merry Christmas, Laurie would have had bonfires and skyrockets if he had had his way.

Hannah "felt in her bones" that Christmas was going to be an unusually fine day, and she proved herself a true prophetess, for everybody and everything seemed bound to produce a grand success. To begin with, Mr. March wrote that he should soon be with them. Beth felt uncommonly well that morning, and dressed in her mother's gift—a soft crimson robe—was borne in triumph to the window to behold the offering of Jo and Laurie. Like elves they had worked by night. Out in the garden stood a stately snow maiden, crowned with holly, bearing a basket of fruit and flowers in one hand, a great roll of new music in the other, a perfect rainbow Afghan round her chilly shoulders, and a Christmas carol issuing from her lips, written on a pink paper streamer. It began:

God bless you, dear Queen Bess!
    May nothing you dismay,
But health and peace and happiness
    Be yours, this Christmas Day.
Here's fruit to feed our busy bee,
    And flowers for her nose;
Here's music for her pianee,
    An afghan for her toes.

How Beth laughed when she saw it, how Laurie ran up and down to bring in the gifts, and what ridiculous speeches Jo made as she presented them!

"I'm so full of happiness that if Father were only here, I couldn't hold one drop more," said Beth, sighing with contentment as Jo carried her off to the study to rest after the excitement, and to refresh herself with some of the delicious grapes from the snow maiden.

"So am I," added Jo, slapping the pocket wherein reposed a long-desired book.

"I'm sure I am," echoed Amy, poring over the engraved copy of the Madonna and Child, which her mother had given her in a pretty frame.

"Of course I am!" cried Meg, smoothing the silvery folds of her first silk dress, for Mr. Laurence had insisted on giving it.

"How can I be otherwise?" said Mrs. March gratefully, as her eyes went from her husband's letter to Beth's smiling face, and her hand caressed a brooch woven from strands of golden, chestnut, and dark brown hair from her daughters.

Now and then, in this workaday world, things do happen in the delightful storybook fashion, and what a comfort that is. Half an hour after everyone had said they were so happy they could only hold one drop more, the drop came. Laurie opened the parlor door and popped his head in quietly. His face was so full of suppressed excitement and his voice so treacherously joyful that everyone jumped up, though he only said, in a breathless voice, "Here's another Christmas present for the March family."

Before the words were well out of his mouth, he was whisked away somehow, and in his place appeared a tall man, muffled up to the eyes, leaning on the arm of another tall man, who tried to say something and couldn't. Of course there was a general stampede, and for several minutes everybody seemed to lose their wits. Mr. March became invisible in the embrace of four pairs of loving arms. Jo disgraced herself by nearly fainting away. Mr. Brooke kissed Meg entirely by mistake, as he somewhat incoherently explained. Amy, the dignified, tumbled over a stool, and, never stopping to get up, hugged her father's boots in the most touching manner. Mrs. March was the first to recover herself, and held up her hand with a warning, "Hush! Remember Beth!"

But it was too late. The study door flew open, the little red wrapper appeared on the threshold, joy put strength into the feeble limbs, and Beth ran straight into her father's arms. After that, the full hearts overflowed, washing away the bitterness of the past and leaving only the sweetness of the present.

A hearty laugh set everybody straight again, for Hannah was discovered behind the door, sobbing over the fat turkey, which she had forgotten to put down when she rushed in from the kitchen. Then the two invalids were ordered to repose, which they did, by both sitting in one big chair and talking hard.

Mr. March told how he had longed to surprise them, and how, when the fine weather came, he had been allowed by his doctor to take advantage of it, how devoted Brooke had been, and how he was altogether a most estimable and upright young man. Mr March paused a minute just there, and after a glance at Meg, who was violently poking the fire, looked at his wife with an inquiring lift of the eyebrows.

There never *was* such a Christmas dinner as they had that day. The

Of course there was a general stampede,
and for several minutes everybody seemed to lose their wits.

fat turkey was a sight to behold, stuffed, browned, and decorated. So was the plum pudding, which melted in one's mouth. Likewise the jellies, in which Amy reveled like a fly in a honeypot. Everything turned out well, which was a mercy, Hannah said, "For my mind was so flustered, mum, that it's a merrycle I didn't roast the pudding, and stuff the turkey with raisins."

Mr. Laurence and his grandson dined with them, also Mr. Brooke— at whom Jo glowered darkly, to Laurie's infinite amusement. Two easy chairs stood side by side at the head of the table, in which sat Beth and her father, feasting modestly on chicken and a little fruit. They told stories, sang songs, "reminisced," as the old folks say, and had a thoroughly good time. A sleigh ride had been planned, but the girls would not leave their father, so the guests departed early, and as twilight gathered, the happy family sat together round the fire.

"Just a year ago we were groaning over the dismal Christmas we expected to have. Do you remember?" asked Jo, breaking a short pause which had followed a long conversation about many things.

"Rather a pleasant year on the whole!" said Meg, smiling at the fire.

"I think it's been a hard one," observed Amy, watching the light shine on her ring with thoughtful eyes.

"I'm glad it's over, because we've got you back," whispered Beth, who sat on her father's knee.

"Rather a rough road for you to travel, my little pilgrims, especially the latter part of it. But you have got on bravely," said Mr. March, looking with fatherly satisfaction at the four young faces gathered round him.

"Did Mother tell you?" asked Jo.

"Not much. Straws show which way the wind blows, and I've made several discoveries today."

"Oh, tell us what they are!" cried Meg, who sat beside him.

"Here is one." And taking up Meg's hand, which lay on the arm of his chair, he pointed to the roughened forefinger, a burn on the back, and two or three little hard spots on the palm. "I remember a time when this hand was perfectly smooth, and your first care was to keep it so. It was pretty then, but to me it is much prettier now—for it shows a little history. I'm proud to shake this good, industrious little hand, and hope I shall not soon be asked to give it away." If Meg had wanted a reward for her labor, she received it in her father's approving smile.

"What about Jo? Please say something nice, for she has tried so hard and been so very good to me," said Beth in her father's ear. He laughed and looked across at the tall girl who sat opposite, with an unusually mild expression in her brown face.

"In spite of the curly crop, I don't see the 'son Jo' I left a year ago," said Mr. March. "I see a young lady who pins her collar straight and laces her boots neatly. Her face is rather thin and pale just now, but I like to look at it, for it has grown gentler, and her voice is lower. I miss my wild girl, but if I get a strong, helpful, tender-hearted woman in her place, I shall feel satisfied. I don't know whether the shearing sobered our black sheep, but I do know that in all Washington I couldn't find anything beautiful enough to be bought with the five-and-twenty dollars which my good girl sent me."

Jo's keen eyes were dim for a minute, and her thin face grew rosy in the firelight as she received her father's praise, feeling that she did deserve a portion of it.

"Now Beth," said Amy, longing for her turn, but ready to wait.

"There's so little of her, I'm afraid to say much, though she is not so shy as she used to be," began their father cheerfully, but recollecting how nearly he had lost her, he held her close, saying tenderly, with her cheek against his own, "I've got you safe, my Beth, and I'll keep you so, please God."

After a minute's silence, he looked down at Amy, who sat on the cricket stool at his feet, and said, with a caress of her shining hair, "I observed that Amy ran errands for her mother all the afternoon, gave Meg her place tonight, and has waited on every one with patience and good humor. She has not even mentioned a pretty ring which she wears, so I conclude that she has learned to think of other people more and of herself less, and has decided to try and mold her character as carefully as she molds her little clay figures. I am glad of this, for though I should be proud of a graceful statue made by her, I shall be infinitely prouder of a daughter with a talent for making life beautiful to herself and others."

"What are you thinking of, Beth?" asked Jo, when Amy had thanked her father and told about her ring.

"I read in *Pilgrim's Progress* today how, after many troubles, Christian and Hopeful came to a pleasant green meadow where lilies bloomed all the year round, and there they rested happily, as we do now, before they went on to their journey's end," answered Beth, adding, as she slipped out of her father's arms and went slowly to the piano, "It's singing time now, and I want to be in my old place. I'll try to sing the song of the shepherd boy which the Pilgrims heard. I made the music for father, because I knew he likes the verses."

So Beth softly touched the keys, and in the sweet voice they had never thought to hear again, sang to her own accompaniment the quaint hymn, which was a fitting song for her:

> He that is down need fear no fall,
> He that is low no pride;
> He that is humble ever shall
> Have God to be his guide.

23

AUNT MARCH SETTLES THE QUESTION

LIKE BEES SWARMING AROUND THEIR QUEEN, mother and daughters hovered about Mr. March the next day, neglecting everything to look at, wait upon, and listen to the new invalid, who was in a fair way to be killed by kindness. As he sat propped up in a big chair by Beth's sofa, with the other three close by, and Hannah popping in her head now and then "to peek at the dear man," nothing seemed needed to complete their happiness.

But Laurie went by in the afternoon, and seeing Meg at the window, seemed suddenly possessed with a melodramatic fit, for he fell down upon one knee in the snow, beat his breast, tore his hair, and clasped his hands imploringly, as if begging some boon. When Meg told him to behave himself and go away, he wrung imaginary tears out of his handkerchief, and staggered round the corner as if in utter despair.

"What does the goose mean?" said Meg, laughing.

"He's showing you how your John will go on by-and-by. Touching, isn't it?" answered Jo scornfully.

"Don't say *my John*, it isn't proper or true," but Meg's voice lingered over the words as if they sounded pleasant to her. "Please don't plague me, Jo. I've told you I don't care much about him, and I don't want anything said."

"Something *has* been said. You are not like your old self a bit, and seem ever so far away from me. I do wish it was all settled," said Jo.

"I can't do anything till he proposes, and he won't, because Father said I am too young," began Meg, bending over her work with a strange little smile, which suggested that she did not quite agree with her father.

"If he did propose, you wouldn't know what to say, but would cry or blush, or agree, instead of giving a good, decided no."

"I'm not so silly and weak as you think. I know just what I should say, for I've planned it all, so I needn't be taken unawares. There's no knowing what may happen, and I wish to be prepared."

"Would you mind telling me what you'd say?" asked Jo more respectfully.

"Not at all. You are sixteen now, and my experience will be useful to you by-and-by, perhaps, in your own affairs of this sort. I should merely say, calmly and decidedly, 'Thank you, Mr. Brooke, you are very kind, but I agree with Father that I am too young to enter into any engagement at present. So please say no more, but let us be friends as we were.' "

"Hum, that's stiff and cool enough! But I don't believe you'll ever say it. If he goes on like the rejected lovers in books, you'll give in."

"No, I won't. I shall tell him I've made up my mind, and shall walk out of the room with dignity."

Meg rose as she spoke, and was just going to rehearse the dignified exit, when a step in the hall made her fly into her seat and begin to sew as fast as if her life depended on finishing that particular seam. Jo opened the door with a grim expression which was anything but hospitable.

"Good afternoon. I came to get my umbrella . . . that is, to see how your father finds himself today," said Mr. Brooke, getting a trifle confused as his eye went from one telltale face to the other.

"It's very well, he's in the umbrella rack. I'll get him, and tell it you are here." And having jumbled her father and the umbrella well together in her reply, Jo slipped out of the room to give Meg a chance to make her speech and air her dignity. But the instant she vanished, Meg began to sidle toward the door, murmuring, "Mother will like to see you. I'll call her."

"Don't go. Are you afraid of me, Margaret?" Mr. Brooke looked hurt. Meg blushed up to the little curls on her forehead, for he had never called her anything but Miss March before, and she was surprised to find how natural and sweet it seemed to hear him say her name.

Anxious to appear friendly and at ease, she put out her hand with a confiding gesture, invited him to sit, and said gratefully, "How can I be afraid when you have been so kind to Father? I only wish I could thank you for it."

"Shall I tell you how?" asked Mr. Brooke, holding the small hand fast in his own, and looking at Meg with so much love in the brown eyes that her heart began to flutter, and she longed both to run away and to stop and listen.

"Oh no, please don't. . . . I'd rather not," she said, trying to withdraw her hand, and looking frightened in spite of her denial.

"I won't trouble you. I only want to know if you care for me a little, Meg. I love you so much," added Mr. Brooke tenderly.

This was the moment for the calm, proper speech, but Meg didn't make it. She forgot every word of it, hung her head, and answered, "I don't know," so softly that John had to stoop down to catch the foolish little reply.

He seemed to think it was worth the trouble, for he smiled to himself as if quite satisfied, pressed the plump hand gratefully, and said in his most persuasive tone, "Will you try and find out? I want to know so much."

"I'm too young," faltered Meg, wondering why she was so fluttered, yet rather enjoying it.

"I'll wait, and in the meantime, you could be learning to like me.

"Shall I tell you how?" asked Mr. Brooke,
holding the small hand fast in his own . . .

Would it be a very hard lesson?"

"Not if I chose to learn it, but . . ."

"Please choose to learn, Meg. I love to teach, and this is easier than German," broke in John, getting possession of the other hand, so that she had no way of hiding her face as he bent to look into it.

His tone was properly beseeching, but stealing a shy look at him, Meg saw that his eyes were merry as well as tender, and that he wore the satisfied smile of one who had no doubt of his success. This nettled her. She felt excited and strange, and not knowing what else to do, followed a capricious impulse and, withdrawing her hands, said petulantly, "I don't choose. Please go away and let me be!"

Poor Mr. Brooke looked as if his lovely castle in the air was tumbling about his ears, for he had never seen Meg in such a mood before, and it bewildered him.

"Do you mean that?" he asked anxiously, following her as she walked away.

"Yes, I do. I don't want to be worried about such things. Father says I needn't, it's too soon and I'd rather not."

"Mayn't I hope you'll change your mind by-and-by? I'll wait and say nothing till you have had more time."

"I'd rather you wouldn't," said Meg.

He was grave and pale now, and looked decidedly more like the novel heroes she admired, but he neither slapped his forehead nor tramped about the room as they did. He just stood looking at her so wistfully, so tenderly, that she found her heart relenting in spite of her. What would have happened next I cannot say, if Aunt March had not come hobbling in at this interesting minute.

The old lady had met Laurie as she took her airing, and hearing of Mr. March's arrival, drove straight out to see him. The family was busy in the back part of the house, and she had made her way quietly in, hoping to surprise them. She did surprise two of them, so much that Meg turned scarlet, and pale Mr. Brooke vanished into the study.

"Bless me, what's all this?" cried the old lady with a rap of her cane.

"It's Father's friend. I'm *so* surprised to see you!" stammered Meg.

"That's evident," returned Aunt March sitting down. "But what is Father's friend saying to you? There's mischief going on, and I insist upon knowing what it is," with another rap.

"We were merely talking. Mr. Brooke came for his umbrella," began Meg, wishing that Mr. Brooke and the umbrella were safely out of the house.

"Brooke? That boy's tutor? Ah! I understand now," cried Aunt March, looking scandalized.

"Hush! He'll hear. Shan't I call Mother?" said poor Meg.

"Not yet. I've something to say to you, and I must free my mind at once. Tell me, do you mean to marry Mr. Cook? If you do, not one penny of my money ever goes to you. Remember that, and be a sensible girl," said the old lady impressively.

Now Aunt March possessed in perfection the art of rousing the spirit of opposition in the gentlest people. If she had begged Meg to accept John Brooke, Meg would probably have declared she couldn't think of it; but as she was ordered not to like him, she immediately made up her mind that she would. Already much excited, Meg opposed the old lady with unusual spirit.

"I shall marry whom I please, Aunt March, and you can leave your money to anyone you like," she said, nodding her head with a resolute air.

"Highty-tighty! Is that the way you take my advice, miss? You'll be sorry for it by-and-by, when you've tried love in a cottage and found it a failure."

"It can't be a worse one than some people find in big houses," retorted Meg.

Aunt March put on her glasses and took a look at the girl, for she did not know her in this new mood. Meg hardly knew herself, she felt so brave and independent—so glad to defend John and assert her right to love him. Aunt March saw that she had begun wrong, and after a little pause, made a fresh start, saying as mildly as she could, "Now, Meg, my dear, be reasonable and take my advice. I mean it kindly, and don't want you to spoil your whole life by making a mistake at the beginning. You ought to marry well and help your family. It's your duty to make a rich match."

"Father and Mother don't think so. They like John though he is poor."

"Your parents, my dear, have no more worldly wisdom than two babies."

"I'm glad of it," cried Meg stoutly.

Aunt March took no notice, but went on with her lecture. "Mr. Rook is poor and hasn't any rich relations, has he?"

"No, but he has many warm friends."

"You can't live on friends. Try it and see how cool they'll grow. He hasn't any business, has he?"

"Not yet. Mr. Laurence is going to help him."

"That won't last long. James Laurence is a crotchety old fellow and not to be depended on. So you intend to marry a man without money, position, or business, and go on working harder than you do now, when you might be comfortable all your days by minding me and doing better? I thought you had more sense, Meg."

"I couldn't do better if I waited half my life! John is good and wise, he's got heaps of talent, he's willing to work and sure to get on, he's so energetic and brave. Everyone likes and respects him, and I'm proud to think he cares for me, though I'm so poor and young and silly," said Meg, looking prettier than ever in her earnestness.

"He knows *you* have rich relations, child. That's the secret of his liking, I suspect."

"Aunt March, how dare you say such a thing?" cried Meg indignantly, forgetting everything but the injustice of the old lady's suspicions. "My John wouldn't marry for money, any more than I would. We are willing to work, and we mean to wait. I'm not afraid of being poor, for I've been happy so far, and I know I shall be with him because he loves me, and I . . ." Meg stopped there, remembering all of a sudden that she hadn't made up her mind, and that John might be overhearing her.

"Well, I wash my hands of the whole affair! You are a willful child, and you've lost more than you know by this piece of folly. No, I won't stay. I'm disappointed in you, and haven't spirits to see your father now. Don't expect anything from me when you are married. Your Mr. Book's friends must take care of you. I'm done with you forever."

And slamming the door in Meg's face, Aunt March drove off in high dudgeon. She seemed to take all the girl's courage with her, for when left alone, Meg stood a moment, undecided whether to laugh or cry. Before she could make up her mind, she was taken possession of by Mr. Brooke, who said all in one breath, "I couldn't help hearing, Meg. Thank you for defending me, and Aunt March for proving that you do care for me a little bit."

"I didn't know how much till she attacked you," began Meg.

"May I stay and be happy?"

Here was another fine chance to make the crushing speech and the stately exit, but Meg never thought of doing either, and disgraced herself forever in Jo's eyes by meekly whispering, "Yes, John," and hiding her face on Mr. Brooke's waistcoat.

Fifteen minutes after Aunt March's departure, Jo came softly downstairs, paused an instant at the parlor door, and hearing no sound within, nodded and smiled with a satisfied expression, saying to herself, "She has sent him away as we planned, and that affair is settled. I'll go and hear the fun, and have a good laugh over it."

But poor Jo never got her laugh, for she was transfixed upon the threshold, staring with her mouth nearly as wide open as her eyes. Going in to praise a strong-minded sister for the banishment of an objectionable lover, it certainly *was* a shock to behold the aforesaid lover serenely sitting on the sofa, with the strong-minded sister enthroned upon his knee and wearing an expression of the most abject submission. Jo gasped, as if a cold shower bath had suddenly fallen upon her—for such an unexpected turning of the tables actually took her breath away. At the odd sound the lovers turned and saw her. Meg jumped up, and John said, "Sister Jo, congratulate us!"

That was adding insult to injury—it was altogether too much—and making some wild demonstration with her hands, Jo vanished without a word. Rushing upstairs, she startled the family by exclaiming tragically as she burst into the room, "Oh, do somebody go down quick. John Brooke is acting dreadfully, and Meg likes it!"

Mr. and Mrs. March left the room with speed, and casting herself upon the bed, Jo cried and scolded as she told the awful news to Beth and Amy. The little girls, however, considered it a most agreeable and interesting event, and Jo got little comfort from them. So she went up to her refuge in the garret, and confided her troubles to the rats.

Nobody ever knew what went on in the parlor that afternoon, but a great deal of talking was done, and quiet Mr. Brooke astonished his friends by the eloquence and spirit with which he told his plans and persuaded them to arrange everything just as he wanted it.

The tea bell rang before he had finished describing the paradise which he meant to earn for Meg, and he proudly took her in to supper, both looking so happy that Jo hadn't the heart to be jealous or dismal. Amy was impressed by John's devotion and Meg's dignity, Beth beamed at them from a distance, while Mr. and Mrs. March surveyed the young couple with such tender satisfaction that it was perfectly evident Aunt March was right in calling them as "unworldly as a pair of babies." No one ate much, but everyone looked very happy, and the old room seemed to brighten up amazingly when the first romance of the family began there.

"You can't say nothing pleasant ever happens now, can you, Meg?" said Amy, trying to decide how she would sketch the lovers.

"No, I'm sure I can't. How much has happened since I said that! It seems a year ago," answered Meg, who was in a blissful dream lifted far above such common things as bread and butter.

"The joys come close upon the sorrows this time," said Mrs. March. "In most families there comes, now and then, a year full of events. This has been such a one, but it ends well, after all."

"I hope the next will end better," muttered Jo.

"I hope the third year from this will end better. I mean it shall, if I live to work out my plans," said Mr. Brooke, smiling at Meg, as if everything had become possible to him now.

"Doesn't it seem long to wait?" asked Amy, who was in a hurry for the wedding.

"I've got so much to learn before I shall be ready, it seems a short time to me," answered Meg, with sweet gravity in her face.

"You have only to wait, I am to do the work," said John, beginning his labors by picking up Meg's napkin, with an expression which caused Jo to say to herself with relief as the front door banged, "Here comes Laurie. Now we shall have a little sensible conversation."

But Jo was mistaken, for Laurie came prancing in, overflowing with enthusiasm, bearing a great bridal-looking bouquet for "Mrs. John Brooke," and evidently laboring under the delusion that the whole affair had been brought about by his excellent management.

"I knew Brooke would have it all his own way, he always does. When he makes up his mind to accomplish anything, it's done though the sky falls," said Laurie, when he had presented his congratulations.

"Much obliged for that recommendation. I take it as a good omen for the future and invite you to my wedding on the spot," answered Mr. Brooke, who felt at peace with all mankind, even his mischievous pupil.

"I'll come if I'm at the ends of the earth." Then Laurie asked Jo, "You don't look festive, ma'am. What's the matter?"

"I don't approve of the match, but I've made up my mind to bear it and shall not say a word against it," said Jo solemnly. "You can't know how hard it is for me to give up Meg," she continued with a little quiver in her voice.

"You don't give her up. You only go halves," said Laurie consolingly.

"It never can be the same again. I've lost my dearest friend," she sighed.

"You've got me, anyhow. I'm not good for much, I know, but I'll stand by you, Jo, all the days of my life!" And Laurie meant what he said.

"I know you will, and I'm ever so much obliged. You are always a great comfort to me, Teddy," returned Jo, gratefully.

"Well, now, don't be dismal. It's all right, you see. Meg is happy, Brooke will fly round and get settled immediately, Grandpa will help him, and it will be jolly to see Meg in her own little house. We'll have capital times after she is gone, for I shall be through college before long, and then we'll go abroad on some nice trip or other. Wouldn't that console you?"

"I think it would, but there's no knowing what may happen in three years," said Jo thoughtfully.

"That's true. Don't you wish you could take a look forward and see where we shall all be then? I do," returned Laurie.

And you can see all that in a twinkling if you read Book Two of *Little Women*, "The Sisters Grow Up."